David fought the steering wheel for control.

The car was still chugging forward but slowed ever so slightly. The sand dollar hanging from the rearview mirror swung in a pendulum arc from all the shaking. *Lord, help!* He needed to get out of the line of fire. *I just need more time. Please hold off the waves.*

The road widened and the Hummer sped past them. The gunman turned around, his torso just above the vehicle's roof, until he faced them. This time the car didn't obey David. "We've been hit!" The VW spun sideways, and another gunshot jolted the car. "They're trying to leave us here."

"If we don't get to the evacuation zone before the tsunami hits, we won't get out," Aria said. "You can't outrun—"

"I know," David interrupted. He didn't need to be reminded that if the gunmen didn't kill them first, the tsunami would.

Heather Woodhaven earned her pilot's license, rode a hot air balloon over the safari lands of Kenya, parasailed over Caribbean seas, lived through an accidental detour onto a black diamond ski trail in the Aspens and snorkeled among stingrays before becoming a mother of three and wife of one. She channels her love for adventure into writing characters that find themselves in extraordinary circumstances.

Books by Heather Woodhaven

Love Inspired Suspense

Calculated Risk
Surviving the Storm

SURVIVING THE STORM

HEATHER WOODHAVEN

HARLEQUIN® LOVE INSPIRED® SUSPENSE

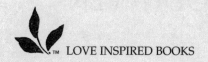

Recycling programs for this product may not exist in your area.

™ LOVE INSPIRED BOOKS

ISBN-13: 978-0-373-44689-6

Surviving the Storm

Copyright © 2015 by Heather Humrichouse

www.Harlequin.com

Printed in U.S.A.

Open rebuke is better than secret love.
—Proverbs 27:5

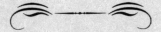

To my children: My favorite characters have names
I almost named you. Thanks for the inspiration.
And if you guess what you were almost called, no complaining.

ONE

Construction dust was going to be the death of her. It was the third time in the past hour the vacuum gagged and sputtered to a stop, but this time it seemed to be serious about staying dead. The crew should have used a Shop-Vac for a preliminary cleaning of the remodeled set of rooms, but Aria Zimmerman suspected they'd skipped that step.

Aria took a swig from the lukewarm water bottle. She could find the new foreman she'd heard had just arrived, or ask her boss, George, for a new vacuum—a stranger versus the man who'd been like a second father to her the past two years. It was no contest.

Aria blew a stray curl off her damp forehead, but it only bounced up and down, tickling her eyelashes. Cleaning in resort areas paid well, but the hard work took its toll. She stood still for a moment in hopes her heart rate would decrease before she tried to talk to George. Thankfully, during her off hours, she sat in her computer networking classes where her sore back could take a much-needed rest.

Aria stared out the window and studied the cliffs in the distance. The beauty beckoned her to call it a day and hike amidst the Sitka spruce trees in the state park, an outcropping on the bluffs above the shore, and listen to the sound of the ocean waves crashing below.

While the state park was only a short distance away, there wasn't easy access unless Aria was willing to cross the creek and climb up the few hundred feet through rocks and weeds. Not feasible. She'd need to drive through town, down the highway, and zig-zag through the winding roads of the park to get to the trailhead.

Since there was already a dusting of snow on the coast, she'd have to settle for a stroll on the beach to loosen her muscles. Sand Dollar Shores was a small town on the Oregon coast, only busy during the tourist season. The unincorporated town didn't have enough funds to handle the slightest flurry of snow. Locals knew enough to put on snow chains or hunker down until it melted, usually within hours.

There were twenty buildings spread out on the property of The Shoreside Conference Center and Resort. The top floor of the main center was fully re-modeled, the last step being carpet, which could only be installed once Aria finished her chore. Her empty water bottle prompted her into action.

She stepped out into the open hallway and leaned over the balcony railing to survey the lobby below. Her stomach dropped at the distance between the two floors. Aria clenched the wood banister underneath her fingers and inhaled. Her new fear of heights took her by surprise at the worst of times.

A wall of windows framed the front of the reception area, displaying the Pacific Ocean. Too bad the dark clouds marred its beauty and, as a result, the lobby's lighting seemed dim as well. If Aria had designed it she would've made the roof curved, without the hard lines and edges that now framed it. A domed ceiling would've allowed for more light.

George walked around the corner of the reception counter, a stack of papers in his hands. Aria opened her mouth to call down to him but stopped when George nodded at someone underneath the balcony. Two men in suits strode into sight, approaching the reception area.

"What was so important, George, that we had to meet in person? I had to cancel two meetings with potential investors. Investors that pay for projects like this. What's the problem?" The man with salt-and-pepper hair shoved his hands into his pockets.

George's chin jutted toward the other suit. "How about you introduce me to your associate first, Robert? I don't believe we've met."

The man named Robert shrugged. "Just a colleague of mine."

Aria's neck tingled. Something didn't seem right. Why wouldn't he introduce the stranger?

"Anything you can say to me, you can say to him," Robert continued. He crossed his arms over his chest. "What about you, George? Anyone else around?"

George straightened, his chest puffed out and his chin held high. Except, at fifty-eight years old, his five-foot-six form dressed in a striped blue-and-white polo and carpenter jeans wasn't the least bit intimidating. Especially when compared to the men in suits. George's eyes lifted over the suits' heads and widened for half a second at the sight of Aria. His features relaxed, but he held her gaze as his lower lip protruded slightly and he shook his head. "No, there's no one here but me."

Aria stepped backward into one of the empty rooms just in case George's gaze would draw the suits' attention. Why had George lied? Was he trying to tell Aria to leave without causing her embarrassment? Or did he want her to listen in? It didn't seem right to eavesdrop, but she also didn't know what else to do without a vacuum. All the construction dust needed to be sucked up before she could mop.

She made her way through the open connecting doorways between rooms. Five rooms down, she peeked into the hallway. She was beyond the balcony and past the risk of interrupting the meeting, yet the way the lobby echoed she could still hear their conversation. She'd listen on the off chance George might want to discuss it later.

During the remodel, they only used natural light from the windows. Aria preferred to avoid the crew, though, and started after they left at three. She had maybe forty minutes to spare before the sunset would force her to pack up for the day.

The housekeeping cart sat right where she had left it. Usually filled with miniature soaps and luxurious bath towels, it was now loaded with heavy-duty cleaning supplies. At least she could start dusting the windowsills. She slipped the orange oil aerosol spray into the pocket of the apron tied around her waist.

Out of the corner of her eye, she spotted a man exiting a guest room farther down the hall. Her heart jolted. She thought she'd been alone on the second floor. She registered the brown steel-toe boots and the leather tool belt as the man walked in the opposite direction, his back to her.

His silhouette reminded her of someone—a stronger, older version of someone she once knew. With his denim button-down shirt and jeans, it had to be the new foreman. No one else on the crew would care enough to wear more than a T-shirt in the humidity, even during winter.

"This is unacceptable!"

Aria stiffened and looked back over her shoulder. Clearly, George's meeting wasn't going as planned. She strained her ears to hear the reply, but the voices had lowered to grumbling. Aria stepped into the shadows, pressed her back against the hallway wall and tiptoed back to the balcony.

"I can't believe you fired my man," the strange voice lectured. "I'm in charge here. That was the stipulation. You keep your hands off."

"You're bamboozling these people, and I won't have it!"

She'd never heard George raise his voice before now. She peeked around the corner to see what was going on. His face had gone pale. The associate held a gun, pointed at George.

Aria's breath caught.

George raised his arms, the papers falling from his hands.

The other man, Robert, shook his head. "Too bad. You and your wife could've been very happy."

Aria's whole body jerked at the sound of a gunshot reverberating through the vaulted ceiling. Her hand shook as she covered her mouth. She couldn't scream, she couldn't cry. Help... She needed to get help. She pressed her back against the wall and fumbled in her pocket for her phone. The movement jostled her apron, and the bearings in the aerosol spray jingled against the aluminum can.

She gasped and her fingers stilled. *Please don't let them have heard that, Lord.*

"Someone's upstairs."

She didn't hear the other man reply. Maybe they'd go away.

Aria strained her ears, but it was hard to hear through her jagged breaths. She heard a creak on the curved stairway at the opposite end of the balcony.

They were coming for her.

Her body betrayed her by shaking. She gritted her teeth in an attempt to stop the chattering. *Think, Aria!* Where could she hide?

The elevator at the opposite end of the hall was shut down and the emergency staircase was unfinished. She looked back to the cleaning cart and remembered where it was usually stored. It was the least inventive hiding place but better than nothing. There was no-where else to run on a floor without furniture. Except it was in the opposite direction she wanted to go. She'd have to run toward the men instead of away.

There was no other way—take the chance or be caught. She darted to the cleaning closet, twisted the doorknob with her right hand and slipped inside. Darkness enveloped her.

Aria clenched her jaw and tightened her fists in an attempt to stop the trembling. The effort only seemed to increase the shakes. The lack of carpet left a dramatic space between the door and the floor. If she turned on her phone, the light would likely seep under the door and alert the man with the gun. Besides, if she talked to a dispatch officer they would hear.

Her mind flashed to memories of the gun... George... She put her hand over her mouth again to prevent a sob. She couldn't afford to fall apart. *Please let him be okay, Lord. I can't lose him too, not after my dad... I just can't go through that again.*

Aria took another shuddered breath. George would want her to focus on staying safe. Who knew what atrocities those men were capable of after what she'd just witnessed? Her eyes acclimated to the low light seeping in from underneath the door.

Footsteps echoed. It almost sounded as if they were in the closet with her, which meant one of the men was likely in the room to her left, searching for her.

Aria began the painful process of a slow turn, careful with each step so as not to produce a creak in the floor joist or another wiggle of the bearings in the dusting can. A metal rod to her right held hangers full of linens. Underneath the rod were stacks of comforters. If she arranged it right and the men weren't looking too hard...

Footsteps pounded—vibrating the entire floor like a miniature earthquake—from the right. She was surrounded and out of time.

"Hey! What are you doing?" a deep voice yelled. "Put the gun down!"

The voice sounded familiar. She bent over and peered out the space underneath the door. The steel-toe brown boots were to the right of the door, and the black wingtips were to her left. Oh, no. The foreman.

Ice-cold dread traveled up her veins. She couldn't watch another man get shot as if his life didn't matter.

"Sorry, buddy, you've seen my face."

Shutting her eyes tight, Aria grabbed the doorknob and lunged with all of her bodyweight, flinging the closet door open as hard as she could, directly into the gunman's body.

A thump confirmed she'd made her target. A sharp crack hurt her ears. The gunshot made contact with the ceiling. She instinctively cowered, her hands over her head. Bits of drywall dropped into her bangs. Strong hands grabbed her right arm. She flinched, but managed to look up at the man she'd just rescued. "David?"

David McGuire's mouth dropped. Aria Zimmerman was not only in front of him, in the flesh, after two years without any contact, but she was the one who'd stopped the man from shooting him.

Unbelievable. What was she doing here, and in the closet?

He shook his head. "There's no time," he said, half to himself. "Come on!"

He gave her upper arm a tug, and the moment he felt her move within his grasp, he let go. She sprinted alongside him down the hall.

When the closet door hit the gunman, it sounded as if she'd hit him with the strength of a linebacker. He doubted her little form could do that much damage, but he also hoped he was wrong because they needed some time to figure out how to get off the second floor.

He headed right for the housekeeping cart. David squinted. Was there anything on the cart that could be used as a weapon? He jerked to a stop for a half a second at the cleaning cart and grabbed a jug of bleach. Now if he could only find—

"What are you doing?" Aria screeched, sliding to a stop.

He looked over his shoulder. The man was on his knees, groaning, one arm pressed over his nose. No doubt that wouldn't last long. "Run ahead of me." Spotting the ammonia, he grabbed it and revised his statement. "Go to the fourth room to the right." They needed to get to the attic he had been inspecting before the sound of a gunshot had prompted him to investigate.

Instead of running down the hallway, Aria slipped into the nearest room. He smirked, sprinting just a step behind her. "Good call." It made more sense to run through the connecting rooms. They wouldn't be as easy to shoot at as they would in the hallway.

"What's in the fourth room?" she asked, huffing.

"Ladder."

She reached the destination and spun around. The ladder had fallen to the ground when he jumped off the third rung, in a hurry to see what the gunshot meant.

"It's not tall enough to get us to the ground if we crawl out the window," she objected. "It's meant for indoor use."

"I know." He kicked the connecting door behind him shut. Aria reached over his shoulder and flipped the dead bolt.

"Set up the ladder to the attic while I rig up these chemicals."

Aria gaped. "You want me to do what?"

David shook his head, rushing to the other door. "You heard me."

"So did I," a cold voice said. The gunman stood in the hallway. His weapon pointed right at David's heart.

TWO

Aria's shoulders drooped. Five more seconds and they would've had that door closed. It wasn't as if bullets couldn't cut through the composite engineered wood, but it would've given them a little more time. Of course, she would've chosen a more resistant white oak or poplar door, but no one had asked her opinion.

Aria's and David's eyes met for the first time in two years. His eyes were the deep sea-green that haunted her dreams. He blinked in acknowledgment. They both turned slowly to face the gunman standing in the doorway. As David twisted, her eyes caught sight of a shiny tool that resembled a giant safety pin. It dangled from the hip pocket of his tool belt—a spark lighter?

Her heart raced. If she could time it right…

"There's no need for guns." David lifted his hands, the chemical jugs hanging from his thumbs. He took a few steps toward the man.

Aria followed his lead, right by his side. She needed to stay in reach of that spark lighter. David must have mistaken her move for wanting to be close to him because he gave her a half smile, his eyes downcast as if apologetic or pitying her. She couldn't decipher which he intended.

"That's far enough," the gunman barked, his voice nasal. He leaned against the left side of the doorway, one hand on the gun and the other arm covering his nose.

Aria kept her head bowed down as if she was cowering, hoping the gunman wouldn't see her as a threat. She peeked up through her bangs.

The man squinted his cold eyes, staring hard at David. "I was going to feel bad having to kill you two, but now not so much." The gunman dropped his arm away from his face. A bloody nose revealed the damage she'd done when she'd shoved the closet door into him.

She slipped her right hand in the front of her apron. Her index finger found the trigger button on the spray can. It was a serious possibility her plan would backfire and injure or kill them all. But if she didn't try, she and David were looking at certain death.

The man wrapped the second hand around the butt of the gun to steady his aim.

Aria pulled out the aerosol can. She prayed it had been shaken enough from running through the rooms. "Drop the gun," she commanded, her voice shaking. She centered her arm toward her target.

The gunman released an ugly laugh. "You gonna dust me to death, lady?"

"No," she croaked. Her left hand popped the spark lighter from David's hip as her right hand sprayed the orange-scented solution in his direction. With one click from the spark lighter, the stream of spray transformed into a flamethrower.

The gunman's left sleeve caught on fire, and he screamed. Aria flung the spray of flames at his other sleeve. He jumped backward, his arm hitting the opposite hallway wall. The gun dropped and slid down the hall. She hurled the spray can into the hallway as well, lest it explode.

"Stop, drop and roll," she shouted at the man. His face contorted into a snarl of rage, but she wasn't trying to be sarcastic. Why wasn't he following her advice? He was on fire!

David rushed past her into the hall. The sound of a gunshot echoed through the hall as he jumped back into the room. He slammed the door closed and flicked the bolt. "I wanted to get the gun, but there's another gunman out there."

"Stop, drop and roll," Aria cried again through the closed door, visions of a burning man searing into her conscience.

David raised an eyebrow. "He'll be fine. It's us I'm worried about. Set up the ladder. Hurry!"

Aria dropped the spark-lighter into her apron and complied but wondered why he couldn't do it himself. She looked over her shoulder to find David on one knee. He placed one jug of ammonia on one end of the hallway door and bleach on the other end. The hallway door shook with pounding.

"There's no way out," the voice said through the door, the one she recognized as Robert. "Save yourself the pain and open up." A moment later a bullet plunged through the bottom panel, mere inches from where David was crouched.

She stumbled backward. "What are you doing?"

"Setting a trap," David answered. "Go on up. I'll meet you in the attic."

Aria surveyed the small square at the top of the ladder. Ever since she had witnessed her dad's fall two years ago, her fear of heights was almost debilitating.

"What are you waiting for? Now!"

A bullet ricocheted off the side of the ladder. Fear of being shot won, and she began to climb. Her feet were heavier than she could remember, but her arms still responded as she pulled herself up each rung and focused on the metal in her hands. She couldn't afford to look up, but she couldn't look down either. Strong hands touched her waist. She jolted and reached for the next rung, glancing down.

"Faster, Aria," he encouraged. "Before the fumes or the bullets get us."

The ladder shook underneath both their weight and she would've stopped but David kept chanting, "Faster, faster." She took solace in the fact that if she slipped, he would, at the very least, cushion her fall.

She shoved the wooden panel at the ceiling up and to the side and crawled onto the nearest two-by-four. A series of three gunshots broke through the wood. She flinched and almost lost her balance.

If she lost her footing, the drywall between the joists wasn't designed to hold weight, and she'd likely fall through the ceiling. Aria let her hands slide along the rough wood as a guide and crawled as fast as she could, trying to make room for David to join her in the attic. The wood vibrated with David's weight. He must've made it.

"Can you stand up?" he asked. "I might need your help."

The hair on the right side of her face flipped up. Something had missed hitting her face by an inch. She felt her eyes widen. Was it a bullet? What if it was something else? Surely, the construction crew would've evicted bats during the remodel.

Aria put one foot in front and pressed up into a lunge until she was upright. She used to be a natural at walking the balance beams of construction, but that was before her dad's death. It was another reminder that her heart, her dreams and her confidence had died with him. Not to mention her relationship with David.

She searched her pockets and found her phone before turning back. The light was enough to see David's face, albeit covered in shadows. He was on his knees, pulling at the ladder rungs like a fisherman pulling in an anchor.

"Smart," she commented.

David didn't reply but grunted with the effort of pulling the heavy metal ladder into the attic. He held up the rest of the ladder's weight with one shoulder, presumably so it wouldn't rest on the drywall spaces.

Aria clicked her smartphone to the flashlight application, set it on the wood behind her and approached. She returned to her knees, leaned over and pulled on the side of the ladder, keeping an eye on David so she could match his pace. His brass-colored hair was cropped short, matching the stubble across his chin and face.

She'd met David while their parents were attending a conference here, a little over seven years ago. She had been eighteen and he was nineteen. They had kept in touch, seeing each other now and then—especially whenever their parents came to Sand Dollar

Shores—but mostly they'd chatted and texted by phone. A couple of years into their friendship they had started to date casually—and long distance at that—he was in California working while she studied in Portland, Oregon.

Sure, they had kissed a few times, but it had never gotten serious over the three years they had dated. Even if it had been serious, that was two years ago—she was twenty-five now, making him twenty-six. She was sure he had moved on, especially given the way things had ended.

She dropped the attic square back in place but her phone's flashlight illuminated the space. David leaned the ladder horizontally against the side of the attic and wiped away the sweat beaded on his forehead.

She took a deep breath, and her nose itched. "We need to find—" her voice cracked "—George. In case there's even a hope he's still alive."

"That was the first gunshot? They shot George?" His hands curled to fists, resting on his hips, and he bowed his head. Aria wondered if his grief matched her own. "Why would anyone want to shoot that man?"

Aria remained silent for a moment, afraid she'd lose control if she spoke. She focused on the light beam and attempted to explain. "George was accusing them of bamboozling people and…and the men wanted him to the look the other way."

"But he didn't." David cocked his head. "Listen. You don't hear gunshots anymore, do you? I'm going to guess the fumes knocked them out. At the very least, they should've been hit with a severe headache or temporary blindness. I figure I bought us about ten minutes."

Her fingers brushed against her phone. "Wait. Have you called the police?"

"Haven't had a chance."

"I'll do it now."

Aria dialed 9-1-1. "It's after five o'clock. That's when they transfer all emergency calls to Beachside. They have a bigger police department."

David paced on the joist, his hands in his pockets. "That's fifteen minutes away," he objected.

She nodded in acknowledgment, but what else could she do? They only had one or two policemen on staff in their tiny town. The bigger towns supplied the majority of manpower. The dispatch answered, and Aria didn't waste any time explaining. "Two gunmen shot a man, and now they're trying to kill us." Aria rattled off the conference center address.

"Where are you now? Are you injured?" the dispatcher asked.

"In the attic. We're not injured…not yet, anyway, but not for their lack of trying."

"Emergency vehicles are en route. There's a pileup on Highway 101. It'll take them a while to clear the road. I'm calling the Summerville sheriff's office to assist. Please hold."

Aria tried to picture Summerville's location. She knew it was south and the last time she'd driven in that direction it'd taken her… "That's got to be a good thirty minutes away," Aria cried.

David shook his head. "Come on. They have our address. We don't have time for this." He flicked on the light from his phone and shoved it in a shallow part of his tool belt so it would still illuminate the attic. He motioned for her to follow him. "Unless you need more space," he quipped, his last word filled with hidden meaning.

A sharp sting in her chest rocked her back to her heels. She bit her lip. Literally backed into a corner, she didn't want to relive that painful time in her life. Her dad had just died, she'd been overwhelmed with handling the arrangements and her mother's grief, let alone her own. Two days later, David had started a text-and-phone-call campaign wanting to know if she had received his card. At the time, it had felt as if he had sent the condolence only to earn brownie points.

Most all of her mother's friends had shown up to give support and casseroles—oodles of casseroles— but Aria's friends showed their love through texts and emails. She understood. It was hard to be around such sorrow in person, and to be honest, she didn't want to be around any of them and be forced to make chitchat. Tons of sympathy cards arrived in the mail, but she had enough to manage without making time to read the stack, his card included. She knew what they all said, anyway. *With sympathy...*

"Yes, I received your card," she had told him on the phone. "But David, I just need some time, some space. This is a little too much for me right now. It's not personal, I just need—"

"If you need space," he had responded, his voice shaking, "then we don't have the kind of relationship I thought we did."

She had been stunned at the emotion behind his voice, but she hadn't known what to do. She hadn't been exaggerating. She really had needed time. The interaction, meant to ease her burden, only made her feel even more alone, something she hadn't thought possible.

Now, in the attic, she stared at him. David held his hands out. "I'm sorry. That was uncalled for."

She nodded, accepting his apology but not sure she could trust herself to comment. His shoulders sagged forward.

"I can carry the ladder myself," he said, "but I'm worried I might knock you over in the process."

She stuck her phone in her pocket, and lifted the back end of the ladder. "You want me to help carry the ladder? I'd be glad to."

David raked a hand through his hair. "We're going to twist the ladder so it's sideways. Think you can carry it under your arm?"

She nodded. The dim light illuminated his form. The past couple of years had widened his shoulders and thickened his already strong arms. David picked up the ladder, waited for her to grab her end and then led the way. Aria put one foot in front of the other. She trained her eyes on the shadowed wooden beam in front of her. "I wish we had more light."

"We'll be across before you know it," he said, his voice lighter. "Good thing I was inspecting the attic today or I might not have known there's an exit at the opposite side. It'll be close to the stairway."

"But then we'll be out in the open."

"If we want to get to George, it's our only hope. Besides, if we stay here, we're sitting ducks."

"Why did George hire you in the first place? He didn't tell me you were coming."

"Yeah, he didn't mention anything about you either," he said, dryly. "He's been calling me the past two weeks. He had suspicions the contractor was using subpar materials."

She gasped. "Subpar?"

David's shadow nodded. "Another reason to watch your step. George was right, and clearly, these gunmen are determined to make sure no one else finds out."

THREE

If David weren't so worried he'd compromise their safety, he'd have released a little of his anger with a punch to one of the two-by-fours he had to crouch under. "Duck," he muttered, not sure if Aria could see the diagonal piece of wood he just passed.

Aria. Why'd she have to be here? It didn't make sense. She should be off at some architecture firm somewhere by now, making the big bucks. What was she doing cleaning? Not that he cared.

Well, at least he didn't want to care. He was just as mortified as she was about that little jibe that came out of his mouth. He was over her, so why did he need to bring it up? He couldn't afford to care, let alone notice she was even more beautiful than the last time he saw her.

As soon as he got them out of this, he'd walk away before she could play with his heart again. Until then, he was in charge. No objections.

"What do you mean, George was right? I didn't think the remodel involved the attic." She groaned. "I should've noticed. The new design added more rooms, so…"

"They had to change the load-bearing walls," he finished. "It was impossible to structure it otherwise. You didn't design this train wreck, did you?"

"No," she said, her voice clipped.

He exhaled loudly. Why was he so bent on antagonizing her? What had come over him? "I didn't think so. George should've asked you to look over the proposals."

"I should've asked," she said, her voice timid. "You're sure the materials they used were subpar?"

"Not just the materials. The engineering. No one factored in the point loads needing to be carried down to the foundation." If it were anyone else besides Aria, he would have put it in simpler terms and said the walls could come tumbling down. Especially if there were an earthquake, as was high probability on the coast— the same risk as Japan, in fact.

Aria groaned. "You…you know where we're going?"

"You don't become foreman at my age without knowing your way around an attic." He cringed the moment he said it. As his family could attest, his ego bristled easily in moments of stress, and his big mouth took over control.

"I know my way around an attic too. What I really want to know is the plan."

He clenched the ladder tighter and took longer strides. He felt the back end of the ladder swing, and Aria shrieked. He froze and twisted so the light shining from his tool belt would find her. "You okay?"

She was straddled across the wood joists set two feet apart. How she managed to move so fast without falling through the drywall was a testament to her time on construction sites.

She gritted her teeth. "Yeah." She blew out a breath. "Could you please keep in mind I have much shorter legs than you?"

It was more an order than a question. "Sorry," he grunted then leaned forward. His pride wanted to make sure she knew what she was missing, and instead it was making him behave insensitively. He needed the Lord's help with his attitude. There was only so much a man could take in one day.

David spotted the raised rectangle two feet ahead on his right. He walked forward until he remembered his maneuver a few seconds ago had almost sent Aria tumbling through the ceiling. "I'm setting the ladder down so I can open our exit."

She didn't respond, but he could feel her movements—through the vibrations of the ladder—mimic his own. He flipped open the exit and took a tentative sniff. He didn't think there were enough chemicals left in the jugs to harm them this far away, but he wanted to be sure. "Clear," he whispered. "To play it safe, we need to be quiet."

They moved in unison, sliding the ladder down through the hole until it made contact with the floor.

"It's going to make noise when we step on it," Aria murmured.

"So let's step fast." David turned around and caught sight of her face, framed in curls. So trusting, so beautiful… He thought she had been perfect for him. He clenched his jaw and looked down. "Let's go."

His foot made contact with every other rung. He reached the floor before Aria was even on the ladder. He rushed to the door leading to the hallway. Past the balcony, he could make out one suit on the hallway floor, his hand over his head. Then where was the other suit?

A gunshot rang from above. Aria screamed. David darted back to the ladder. She slid the rest of the way down, right into his arms. "Are you okay?" he asked. Her T-shirt and khaki pants didn't seem to show any evidence of blood.

She shivered but nodded as she found her footing. "I saw a light on the other side of the attic. It's the Robert guy. He's up there."

"Then we don't have a lot of time." David yanked the ladder down to the ground, grabbed Aria's hand and sprinted for the curved staircase.

"Short legs," she huffed. He let go of her hand but almost came to a complete stop at the sight of George. He was on the tile, on his side, his hand over his heart.

Aria passed David on the staircase and sprinted across the lobby floor. "George," she whispered. She fell to her knees in front of him. "George. Answer me," she begged. "Please!"

David reached her side and kneeled. His friend, and boss for a day, had his eyes closed and looked pale. Even if help arrived within the minute, it didn't look as if he had a chance. David felt for George's pulse on his right hand.

George's eyes fluttered open and darted between David and Aria. The man smirked and closed his eyes again. "Two favorite people," he whispered, his voice hoarse from the strain.

"Help is on the way. We need to get you away from those men. Just hold on." Aria placed her hand on George's left hand, pressing against his gunshot wound. "Help me move him, David."

George licked his lips and opened his eyes again. "No, sweetheart." He took a ragged breath. "I'm ready." His stare moved to David. "My desk." Another breath. "The drive." He sighed. "Make it right." He closed his eyes. "Proud of you."

"I can't lose you, George," Aria said. George didn't move or respond. She turned to David and shook his arm. "Help me! I can't lose him."

The pulse beneath David's fingers disappeared. His shoulders sagged. "We can't save him, Aria." He cleared the emotion from his throat. "He's gone."

She shook her head. "No. George, stay with me." Her voice cracked. Tears filled her eyes.

David's chest burned with restrained agony. He let go of his boss's hand and reached for Aria. He was ashamed he'd ever spoken to her with anything but kindness.

A thump reverberated from above. In his peripheral vision, he spotted a flash of black approaching the balcony. The gunman had jumped from the attic. David shoved Aria down to the ground as a bullet crashed through the twenty-foot-high front window of the lobby. A cascade of shattered glass dropped to the floor.

His eardrums seared with the pain of such a violent crash, but his first priority was Aria's safety. He jumped over her, grabbed her arm and slid her crouched form across the floor until they were past the corner of the reception counter. He ducked as a series of bullets lodged in the wall behind him. "This guy's nuts!"

Aria's wide eyes and shallow breathing grabbed

his focus. He put his hands on her shoulders. "Aria. Are you okay?"

She shook her head. "No," she whispered. She blinked and, as she inhaled, pulled her shoulders back as if she'd put on armor. "But I know we have to go. I think I know the way out."

She slithered past him and into a closet. At least he thought it was a closet, judging by the pillows and blankets in the cubbies lined against the wall. But once inside, he spotted two doors. The door to the right was marked Conference Room, but the door to the left simply said Management. Aria stood and flung the left open. Of course. George's office—and George had his own private entrance. Or exit, in this case.

David locked the office door behind him, then crossed the room to open their escape route. Aria had taken to rifling through George's desk drawers.

"What are you doing? The guy's got to be clear across the lobby by now."

She ignored him. Rage filled his veins. Every second increased their chances of being shot. "I can't keep you safe if you don't—"

"Got it." She thrust a thumb drive up in the air. "I think this is what he wanted us to find." She lowered her hand and stared at the drive. "It's got to be."

David lunged for her wrist. "We leave now." He pulled her out of the building. The wind rushed past him, the snowflakes melting on his skin. The conference center campus was placed diagonal to the coast's jagged shoreline. Half of the buildings were built on a hill, above the main conference lodging. It ensured every building had at least partial access to an ocean view. His truck was attached to a trailer full of tools at the opposite end of campus. "Where's your car?"

Her eyes, dark with worry, surveyed the area. "Parked near the cottages, next to the garden. If we run across the parking lots with him after us, we'll be target practice."

She was right but he didn't have any other solution. He shook his head. "We don't have a choice. My truck is too far away—"

She grabbed his arm, her eyes widening. "The caves."

David whipped his gaze to the ocean. "Is it low tide?"

Her curls blew across her face. "No." She started running. He pumped his arms to catch up as he heard her say, "But it's not high tide yet either."

He blew out a breath. Could the day possibly get any worse? Side by side they tore through the wet sand. Only ten feet until shelter. Just as they rounded the corner of the nearest rocky cliff another gunshot rang out. A sting ran across his right shoulder and wet warmth ran down to his elbow. David heard his own cry before he fully registered what had happened. His shoulder had been hit but they couldn't afford to slow their pace. He ran harder, his thoughts fueling his rage. The anger helped tame the pain.

A nearby wave crashed beside him, and a moment later the ripples hit their feet. It was harder to keep up a fast pace, especially in his boots. They were sinking into the sand. Aria jabbed a finger past his face and came to a stop. He turned to follow her gaze. A thin crevice.

He looked over his shoulder. The gunman had yet to round the corner. It was now or never. He entered first with Aria right on his heels.

Once again they were in the dark together. The

crevice was tight, especially in the front where the ocean slapped against the face of the cliff. The space opened slightly. Shoulder to shoulder they sloshed through the six-inch-deep ocean water. He gritted his teeth. The air might be in the forties, but the water could only be ten degrees warmer. Only the hardiest of surfers would brave fifty-degree water, even with a wet suit. He had never been one for surfing...or for enjoying cold temperatures.

They couldn't afford to slosh in the water much longer, or their health would suffer. The rock opened up into a small cavity. The sea cave. The air grew stale and musty. He reached out and his fingertips found Aria's shoulder. She stopped walking, but her body shivered underneath his hand. Without a hint of light, they had to stay together.

He sniffed, making sure there weren't any unpleasant smells that might indicate new sea lion territory.

Memories flooded David's mind. Four years ago they had strolled the same beach hand in hand, discussing their dreams for building their own resort similar to the Shoreline Conference Center. Their center would serve as a ministry and provide groups, and most important, families, access to amazing vacations and marriage conferences in beautiful locations they'd otherwise never be able to afford. Exactly like George had done for their own families.

Aria had claimed the designs were already sketched in her mind, and David had boasted his resourcefulness would allow it to be built under budget yet still strong enough to handle the toughest earthquakes and floods. When they had discovered the sea cave that day, years ago, they were just going to check it out and come back to the beach straight away.

But when Aria had heard a sound behind her and jumped into his arms, the darkness had given him the courage to kiss her forehead…and then her lips for the first time. She had reciprocated with such a fierce, passionate kiss of her own that he had been completely ignorant of the approaching high tides.

David cleared his throat, hoping to clear the memories with it. "Are you sure about this, Aria? Last time we both barely got out."

Aria fought to keep her head on straight. She had almost let the grief take over in the lobby; she couldn't afford for it to get a foothold again. "I know," she admitted. "And with a lot of scratches to boot."

He winced but she had a feeling it wasn't from the memory. "Are you okay?"

"Yeah. The sting in my shoulder is getting worse. It caught me off guard. I wasn't dealing with a bullet wound last time we were in the cave."

"You weren't shot." Her teeth chattered the moment she opened her mouth.

"I'm pretty sure the hot blood running down my arm isn't from the snow."

"I know," she responded, her voice softer but still shaking. "I saw it happen. I'm sure it hurts, but he shot the side of the cliff, and the rock broke off and…"

"Hit me," David finished. "So I'll live."

"I hope it didn't do as much damage as a bullet. It was too close, though." Unbidden images of the last time they found themselves in the cave filled her mind. He was right. They had barely escaped and now he was…thicker. "I am beginning to wonder if we should've opted for taking our chance in the parking lots," she said and reached out to find him. Her fingertips found his denim shirt—presumably his chest, judging by how tall she knew him to be. It was maddening to be in the dark and not be able to turn on a light. She moved her hands apart, searching, until they found his arms.

"Uh… Aria, what are you doing?"

"Don't worry. I'm not trying to cuddle." She slid her hands up and over the outside of his arms, careful to only touch the front of his shoulder to avoid his injury. "It's just that you're…well, much wider than last time."

"All part of the job," he blurted out.

Aria knew manual labor built solid men, but her own father was never so broad. "I guess," she replied. "I'm a little worried you won't fit anymore." Another rush of water flooded in and soaked the back of her knees. Her hands shook from the chill. David was much taller, but the wave had to have reached the middle of his shins. He had to be feeling the effects of the cold water as well.

"Maybe we should double back," David suggested. "He could be gone by now."

"What if the other gunman sees us?"

"Fine. We try the tunnel, but you've made me a little concerned that I might get stuck. If I so much as feel rock scraping my shoulder, I'm backing out. Want me to pull out my phone?"

They heard a slap of water, then another. It didn't sound like waves. Was the gunman in the cave? Surely not. He'd be in the same predicament they were. He was likely outside of it, though. Instinct prompted Aria to reach her hands out and find David's.

Her hands moved over his wrist. She felt his hot breath on her forehead and wanted to jump a foot back but remained frozen. They both stood still—aside from their shivering—and quiet. Each minute seemed like an hour in the frigid water. When she was confident she didn't hear any more slaps, it was all she could do not to run out of the cave. But even if she tried, she knew the force of the incoming tide would bounce them around the small rocky entrance. They wouldn't make it back out without getting slammed into the rock walls.

They needed to find the tunnel now. Because every other option meant severe injury…or worse.

FOUR

David moved only when the tide surged, in case there was a gunman waiting outside, listening. He doubted there'd be anyone, though, judging by the depth of the water. High tide was coming fast.

Aria's hand remained on his wrist, pulling. Her slow movements complemented each gush of water. She was graceful, just as she had been the last time they thought they were doomed. Only then, they had used their phones to find the other exit, and didn't have two men out to kill them.

She grunted and jerked his wrist up a foot. Ah, she'd found the ledge. He climbed up after her, relieved to be out of the water. She spun around, trembling. David pulled her in close and squeezed his arms around her. "You're freezing."

He felt her nod against his chest, but the shaking lessened only a bit. His heart was certainly shaking more, though.

"They can't see us now unless they come all the way in," she whispered. He didn't trust himself to answer. His shoulder stung. He was angry at the situation and confused by this woman that still made his heart ache.

She tugged on his wrist again, then let go. He missed her touch the moment she left. A small glow erupted from her hand. Her phone was on, but she was covering most of the screen with her other hand. It was enough to see the second crevice deep within the cave. The one they would need to escape. Shuffling, they made their way through. So far, so good.

"Duck," she ordered.

He dropped to his knees, the hard, slimy rock pressing into his palms. Yes, he remembered this place well, but mostly the kisses, not the emergency exit route. His shoulder chose that moment to smart again. The frustration returned and he almost welcomed it—maybe it'd help keep him focused. His fingers accidentally brushed against her calf. Her skin felt like ice.

"Why'd you stop moving?" he asked.

"I wanted to make sure you were okay." Her voice was husky, filled with emotion. She had to be thinking about George again. Aria was a smart woman, brilliant—a visionary even—but she led with her heart more often than logic, and she kept it all to herself until she burst. He loved the way her mind worked during the times she did open up, but he could never anticipate when an emotional tidal wave was coming and would take charge.

He suspected it was the exact reason she'd said she needed space after she got his card. He still hated himself for telling her his feelings through a love letter. He'd intended for it to be romantic, though, and a keepsake she would cherish and show their children someday. He scoffed. A bad decision only trumped by their phone conversation shortly after she said she'd received it.

He had expected her to gush with returned feelings of love and instead she'd said she needed space. The word still made him cringe, but hanging up on her had effectively closed any chance they had at a future. He'd tried to apologize in person, driving the six hours from his job in Northern California to Portland, only to find her gone from her apartment. He didn't give up, though, until he found her parents' house also empty, a for-sale sign posted in their yard.

And now he was letting his own feelings cloud his thoughts.

"Keep moving," he pressed. "I'll tell you if I'm not fine."

"That sharp curve and rise is coming."

He took a deep breath. Last time they'd emerged with long lacerations etched on their foreheads. They'd been prescribed healthy doses of penicillin. Their parents, there for a Christian construction workers conference, had lectured them both, despite the fact that David was a twenty-two-year-old man at the time. When he had pointed that tidbit out, his mother snapped, "Once a parent, always a parent."

David supposed the darkness wasn't helping keep the memories at bay. He trailed her and tried to keep his head down low in preparation for the curve. A flicker of light crossed the surface of the rock directly underneath his hand. They were almost out. "If those guys don't kill us, when our parents find out we did this again, they're going to want to try."

She remained silent—either she hadn't heard him or she didn't think his attempt at humor was funny. He pressed forward until he saw the sky.

Aria was already above him, facing him on her

hands and knees, looking down into the tunnel. She slapped what resembled a tree root that dangled in front of him. His shoulder ached as he pulled himself up and collapsed onto the long grasses. Drizzle hit his face. The snow had turned to a sprinkle of cold rain. They were perched on a small overhang covered in tufts of beach grass, the rest of the cliffs behind them.

David needed a moment to catch his breath.

"I never thought we'd do that again," Aria murmured.

"I don't think we should make it a tradition."

She cracked a half smile and threw a thumb over her shoulder. "That path is still there, around the corner. I think it'll wind us behind some of the buildings and, if I remember right, get us a lot closer to the cottages." She lifted her face and closed her eyes as if welcoming the drizzle. Her eyes flashed open, and she groaned. "But we'll have to find a place to cross the creek."

"I'm really getting sick of water." He jumped up. His shoulder throbbed but seemed to have stopped bleeding. The path was easy to find and, to their advantage, hugged the cliff's edge. The tall beach grass and boulders outlining the dirt would act as good hiding spots should the men still be scouting for them. Over their heads was the state park. It was an outcropping of forest that sat almost like a floating peninsula above the coast.

They took turns stepping over a chain that hadn't been there years before. It held a metal sign that read Restricted. Aria squeezed her hands together, the distress evident on her face. The state park likely deemed the trail unsafe, but it was safer than facing the gunmen. It'd have to do. He plowed forward, determined to get to the cottages in record time.

"David!" Her body slammed into his back.

Aria knew David's physique was different since the last time she'd seen him but now her sore cheek attested to the rock-solid change. She patted his back. "Sorry. I'm fine. Just slipped."

"I hope no one heard you," he grunted before continuing.

She pursed her lips. Apparently, he'd turned into quite the charmer in the past couple of years. The nice boy she'd held hands with was clearly long gone. She couldn't help but wonder what had happened to change him so much. What had been going on in his life after he broke up with her?

Aria took a tentative step on the next black rock, before lurching down and stumbling once again into his back. He huffed. "Would you like to save some time and use my back as a punching bag?"

"It was an accident," she objected. "Are you angry with me?" She put her hands on her hips. In her mind, he had no right. She was trying to be nice without rehashing the past, but it wasn't working. The man had a chip on his shoulder, and she wasn't referring to the rock that had hit him. And with George gone and two men trying to kill them—

David stilled for a short moment but didn't turn around. "No, I'm not angry with you," he muttered. "I'm angry at the situation. Please bear with me, Aria. I'm having a hard time with all of this. I don't mean to take it out on you."

Her eyes blurred again. She needed to think about

something else before she started crying, for she feared that once she started she wouldn't be able to stop. Never had she ever felt so alone, and that was saying something.

She stared at the back of David's head. His hair used to be as curly as her own locks. Now, it looked trimmed—wavy, but no curls. The lower half of his face was covered with the same brassy dark blond hair. The beard made him look older, as well as the extra bulk his shoulders sported.

"Did…did you grow the beard for the job?"

He spun and raised an eyebrow.

"To look older?"

He shrugged and moved forward.

"Please," she said. "We don't have to be friends, but I need…I need to talk to keep my mind…"

"I get it," he said, his voice softer. "Yes. The beard helped. When you're one of the youngest on the crew, you need to earn their respect to lead them."

"So it's rare to be young and be foreman?"

He nodded. "My construction management degree came in handy."

She smiled. "You went back to school? I thought you had an automatic job with your dad."

"Mom encouraged me to get some extra experience outside of Dad's crew."

She'd always liked David's mom. It seemed like smart advice. "Living the dream, then?"

He grunted a noncommittal response. "What about you?" He leaned up against the side of the rock wall for a moment and surveyed the layout of the land. "What's up with the cleaning?"

Her spine tingled. She hadn't expected the conversation to turn personal, and she was a little bit embarrassed to share with him her career decision. She had a feeling he wouldn't agree. And unlike George, who'd also questioned her choice, David wouldn't quietly respect her new direction. She'd no doubt have to hear his thoughts on the matter and she wasn't sure she could endure that just yet.

David continued down the path. She lurched again onto yet another rock and decided the best route was to keep it short and simple. "I took a break from school for a while. Now I'm back. Cleaning pays the bills."

He narrowed his eyes and studied her for a moment, as if expecting she'd say more, but she didn't reward him.

"So why didn't George tell me you were here when he hired me?" he asked. "You'd think he could've mentioned that little tidbit, unless someone had asked him to keep it quiet."

"I told you, he kept me in the dark too." David had a point, though. When she had reconnected with George over a year ago, he'd asked after David. And she'd told him, in detail, about how their relationship ended. George had known it would be awkward for both of them and yet he kept it to himself. She huffed.

David's gaze darted behind her and down the hill. "What? Did you see something?"

"No. Sorry. I just realized George was trying to play matchmaker." She spotted a white tail bouncing up the boulders. This area of the coast had wild bunnies. They were a treat for visitors ever since she could remember. A rustle in the grasses revealed more bunnies, bounding up their way.

"Wonder why they're all coming this way," David

mused. He pointed to a bend in the creek. "Think we can make it over on those boulders?"

If her shoes weren't sopping wet, it'd be a piece of cake. She steeled her nerve. "I can manage."

David lengthened his stride. "Barbara was the matchmaker, wasn't she? Didn't she set up your mom and dad?"

Aria cringed. He was hitting all the painful memories today. "Yes. Did you know Barbara passed away?"

He jutted his chin out. "Yeah."

"Did you know George remarried last year?"

"Yes, but I haven't met her yet. What's she like?"

Trophy wife came to mind, as well as *gold digger*. The woman was probably twenty…maybe thirty years younger than George. "Uh. George loves—loved her. I know that much."

"That's all you can tell me?"

"I was raised if you don't have something nice to say…"

David turned and raised an eyebrow. "Point taken." He sighed. "We should warn her in case those men come after her. Do you have her number?"

Her face burned. She should've thought of that first. George would've wanted her to make sure Valentina was safe. "No," she admitted.

David reached out for her hand and together they crossed the creek one boulder at a time. The first boulder was easier than she thought aside from a little slipping, which he helped remedy. He let go of her hand and crossed to the second boulder.

"It's farther than I thought. Can you reach?"

Aria didn't answer but focused on her destination and stepped out. Unfortunately, he was right to be concerned. The front of her toe reached the rock, but she was uncomfortably straddled…and stuck. David grabbed her waist and pulled, and she found herself in his arms. "Thank you," she murmured. The remaining boulder she crossed without incident, but she was thankful when her squishy shoes touched dry land.

"How long since you called the police?"

She consulted her phone. "Assuming the pileup is still an issue, I'm guessing Summerville police are still…ten or fifteen minutes out?"

He blew out a long breath. "That long? Let's get to your car before they spot us."

"Except I don't have my car keys with me. They're in my room." There were fifteen other buildings on campus still waiting for their turn to be remodeled. Thankfully, George had let her stay for free in one of the units.

He put his hands on his hips. "Your room?"

"I'm staying in one of the cottage units," she continued. "The men probably don't even know I stay on campus. We could grab the keys or just hide inside until the authorities show up."

"Assuming we can get there without being seen." He placed a hand on her back and shoved her down into the long grasses. "Get down!"

FIVE

Aria fell flat on her stomach. David flattened right next to her as if he was sliding into home base. She turned her face away as the sand sprayed. "What is it?"

"I think I just spotted the guy you torched. I don't think he'll take kindly to seeing you again."

She pressed up on her elbows, her eyes peering through the blades, like a cat on the hunt. "You're the one who fumed him unconscious. I doubt he'd take kindly to seeing you again either." She squinted. The man carried a giant red jug. "What's he doing?"

"Looks like gas cans. I'd say he's preparing to torch the center."

She dropped her forehead into sandy hands and prayed the authorities would be able to stop him. The tall grasses rustled all around her. She jolted as fur brushed against her arms. "More bunnies." She peeked up. They were all bounding for the rocks, up into the state park.

"Something must've spooked them. I can't imagine they're running from the men unless they've already started a fire." He groaned. "I was thankful there weren't any tourists around when they were trying to shoot us, but now, I'm wishing for some more people to help us."

The wind gust whipped the long grasses against their heads and sprayed a layer of sand against her arms. "David, if the conference center is on fire, the rest of the campus is going to go up in flames. One building at a time—like dominoes."

His hand still rested on her back, the heat from it making it hard for her to focus. "We're not waiting around for that to happen. Start crawling."

Twenty feet ahead was the corner of the cottage labeled the Skipper's Quarters. Once behind that, they would be safe from view until the cottages. Her throat burned. It was George's home, back when Barbara was still alive. His new wife, Valentina, insisted they live off campus, though, and he'd obliged. "At least we know Valentina isn't here."

"Good. How do we know that?"

"I don't where they live, only that it's not here anymore." Her knees stung from the occasional pebble she crossed. "Ready?"

He nodded.

She straightened and sprinted. A hundred feet more and they'd be safe behind the Bible Study Lodge. She looked to David. He wasn't nearly out of breath as she was, his long legs taking one stride for every two of her quick feet.

She rounded the corner and pressed her hands on top of her knees to catch her breath. "One more parking lot to cross."

David looked over his shoulder. "Clear."

She took a deep breath, and they were sprinting again. At her door, she slipped the card into the lock and the light flashed green. She dashed inside, David directly behind her. The walls around her provided a sense of safety, even if it was false, and she felt her guard weakening. She slumped to the ground. Her heart beat so hard and fast against her throat that nausea overwhelmed her. "I think I'm dying," she said between gulps of air. Her hand flew to her mouth at the realization of what she'd just said. How could she be so insensitive? The events of the past half hour broke her. Her breath turned jagged, fighting to hold back sobs that threatened.

David's knees dropped in front of her. "Oh, Aria." He patted her shoulder clumsily.

"It's such a stupid expression."

"I know. I say it, too. It's okay. We both need time to process, but unfortunately, we can't afford that right now, honey."

Her gaze flew to meet his from the term of endearment. Was he blushing?

David continued. "I don't think we can afford to wait here for the cops when we don't know how long it'll take them. Can you tell me where your keys are and I'll get them?" He stood up and looked around the room—everywhere, it seemed, but at her.

"No. I'll get them." She stood up, her heart still in her throat from the physical exertion. She walked past the living room into the small kitchenette. Her black purse sat on the counter. She rifled in it until she came across the jingling set. She slung the purse strap diagonally, and cringed at the sensation of her wet clothes stuck to her skin.

The framed family picture on her shelf caught her eye. It had been a gift from George when she first arrived. George had no idea the picture on the beach had been the last photo taken of her with her parents until he presented it. If there was a chance the building was going to catch on fire, she didn't want this photo to go with it.

David noted Aria's demeanor change when she picked up a framed photograph with great care. He couldn't see who was in the photograph—a boyfriend perhaps? He hoped it was a family photograph, which prompted his desire to ask after her parents. They used to be good friends with his own parents, but his mom said they hadn't heard a word from the Zimmermans ever since David cut ties with Aria. That had surprised him, as Aria's father didn't seem to be the type of guy to allow that to affect a long friendship.

Her dad was a man David genuinely respected, one of the men he hoped to emulate when starting his own business. He wanted to find a way to ask or peek at the photograph, but he had no right and he supposed it wasn't the time to have such a conversation. David followed her into the kitchen and cleared his throat. "We need to go in case they succeed in starting a fire."

Her eyes widened. "Computer!" She dropped the frame into her purse, spun and ran into the bedroom. "We need to check George's thumb drive."

"And we can do that as soon as I get you somewhere safe!" He clenched his jaw, angry with himself for letting her take her time. They should be far away by now.

She emerged from the hall. He recognized the silver behemoth of a laptop. She had received the computer as a present when she went away to college years ago.

Her parents had it outfitted with the expensive engineering software she would need for her architecture courses. It was an out-of-date beast now.

Aria struggled to shove it in her purse. He blew out a breath. "Aria, just let me take it. We're risking our lives standing around."

She raised her eyebrows, and he knew it was a losing battle. Once she'd decided to do something there was no deterring her. They were both stubborn. They only chose to be obstinate about different things.

"I'm calling the police for a new ETA." He raised the phone to his ear, but the floor started to shake. He struggled to stay upright.

The phone crashed to the ground. Aria's eyes widened as she fell backward, her hands gripping the laptop.

He lunged for her and grasped her elbows but barely kept her standing as his own balance was put to the test. The lamp on the end table crashed to the ground. Little bits of drywall dropped from the ceiling like snowflakes.

The earthquake was stronger than any he had experienced in the past, and as a California boy, that was saying something. He looked into Aria's wide eyes. "Drop!" They both hit their knees and crawled across the littered floor. He squeezed underneath the thin entry table lining the wall next to the door and made sure there was room for her. She set the laptop down beside her and grabbed the outside leg of the table. David followed suit and grabbed the opposite leg.

Crash!

David groaned. The beautiful flat-screen television

had smashed to the ground, leaving a gaping hole in the wall.

A rumbling boom in the distant grew closer, almost as if thunder had rolled across the coast. Aria's wide eyes searched his face. "What was that?"

"It could be the conference building," he said, hoping he was wrong. At least it was the only building that had been remodeled under the previous foreman's direction. After David's initial inspection he had hoped to ask George how he would know if the crew left behind were part of whatever shady dealings that had occurred. Now he'd never know the answer.

David also wondered how his truck was faring parked next to the storage shed—also not the most stable workmanship he'd ever seen. This had to be the worst day of his life thus far, and he prayed he'd never experience worse. He had driven all day from his old job in Northern California to take over as foreman for the center's remodel. In fact, he'd been on site for only an hour before the shooting.

But what would've happened had he turned George down and never come? Would Aria have been left alone to face the murderers? Would she still be alive without him? His chest ached at the thought. The gunmen were still out there, and he needed to get Aria to a safe location.

He slid his hand out from under the covering of the flimsy table and grabbed his fallen phone. Despite a crack down the front of the glass, it seemed to be in working order.

After he dialed 9-1-1 for a second time, the phone emitted a series of beeps before a computerized voice informed him, "All circuits are busy. Please try your call again."

He groaned. "Try your phone."

Aria fumbled in her purse for a second but within moments came to the same conclusion. "Network is overloaded. Always happens when there's an earthquake." Her mouth dropped. "That's why all the rabbits were heading for the state park. Instinct."

He'd agree with her, but it seemed odd to him that the rabbits were heading for higher ground. He shrugged. "That settles it. We have no guarantee that help is around the corner anymore. Let's go before any aftershocks can happen, assuming the roads are okay. For all we know, with an earthquake of that magnitude there could be rockslides on the highway. Where's your car?"

"Right around the corner, next to the garden."

He nodded, scrambled out from under the table and flung the door open. Aria had her suitcase of a purse slung over her form diagonally. A third of the laptop stuck out, but she still managed to sprint past him. Thankfully the snow and rain mix had stopped. He matched her speed but came to a crashing halt when he spotted the only car in the parking lot facing the gardens. "You still have the Bug?"

The baby blue Volkswagen Beetle made him cringe just looking at it. His knees would need to shove into his chest to lower himself into one of those, but it fit Aria and her cheerful personality.

She nodded, the pink hues from the setting sun illuminating her hair. He looked above her head. The middle of the conference center roof resembled a bowl. His jaw clenched. Needless destruction.

Aria followed his gaze. "You were right," she whispered. "It caved. I'm so thankful we got out of there in time." She sniffed, prompting him to do the same. Had they started the fire?

"David, do you smell something?"

SIX

Aria's mouth filled with the taste of burnt rubber. "They lit the center on fire, didn't they?"

"I'm not sure. I don't smell anything yet." David put a hand on her shoulder, and a small shiver went up her spine. "Either way, let's get out of here."

She took a step away from his touch and fumbled for her car keys. David put his hand over hers and stilled her shaking fingers. She looked up at him. How could he look so good despite everything? Aria was positive she had bits of insulation in her hair and probably wet seaweed on her face from the cave. Her only hope of not looking like a drowned rat was the setting sun.

On him, the purple and orange hues hit his face in a way that only highlighted his best features—his lips, his eyes and the new definition in his arms. She hadn't forgotten how well he kissed, and the time in the cave only refreshed her memory all too well.

"I'll drive," he said and slipped the keys from her fingers.

She let him take the keys without an argument. "It'll be dark within a few minutes," she muttered.

A high-decibel wail vibrated her eardrums to the point of pain. Aria clamped her hands over her ears.

David spun around. "Is that what I think it is?"

Her mouth gaped open. No, it couldn't be. The wail continued. "A tsunami warning!" Aria's stomach clenched and wouldn't let go. If the men, the fire or the tsunami didn't kill her first, the stress and fear would do the job.

David ran to her. "Time to leave." The warning siren released another series of high-pitched wails.

"Wait! Who's going to stop them? The police won't come now! We can't just let them get away with this."

David squinted, his eyes hard. "The tsunami warning says otherwise."

He was right, of course, but she hated it. She wished she could do something, anything. David reached for her arm and stiffened. "I see flames. That Robert guy is in between the buildings. I think he spotted me." He tugged on her elbow. "Come on!"

Her soggy shoes made slapping noises against the matted grass as they cut across the garden to her car. If Robert had spied them, he would only have to follow the sound.

David ran around to the driver's side. Aria wasted no time hopping in and buckling up. She scanned the area, and while she couldn't see either of the men in suits, the spiraling black smoke from behind the cottages meant the fire was spreading. "Where's that snow and rain when you need it?"

David cranked the ignition and spun the steering wheel so fast they whipped around one hundred eighty degrees, ready to drive east, directly away from the ocean. He frowned, momentarily frozen, his eyes focused on the sand dollar dangling from her rearview mirror. "You kept it?"

She bit her lip, wishing he hadn't seen it, and toyed with the idea of fibbing. Yes, it was the same sand dollar he had found and given her four or five years ago, and yes, she had researched the best way to preserve it, but for all he knew it could've been from one of the tourist shops. "Yes." She shrugged. "It's rare to find one so unblemished. Can we go now?"

Aria pictured the tsunami evacuation brochure. It was the only thing she had to read in the tiny cottage besides the Bible and the takeout menus. She almost had it memorized. "The warning means we have fifteen…forty-five minutes at the max."

He stepped on the gas, and her head flung back into the seat cushion.

"I don't know where I'm going," he admitted.

"The evacuation tower." She pointed to the far corner up the hill. The entire town from the shores to the highway was slanted. If they reached the highway, they would, hopefully, be out of danger and close to help.

But the tower was the safest of all. The community had decided after the tsunami of 1964 that if they ever built a town hall, it would be large enough to hold up to 1500 people and strong enough to withstand thirty-foot tidal waves. Built on post-tensioned concrete beams, it had an open system that allowed the water to flow through without resistance. It cost the state millions of dollars but it held a stash of supplies that could feed and care for a small army. And it'd save lives.

"Think there will be enough room for us?" David asked.

Aria had forgotten David hadn't been back in the

past couple of years. He hadn't seen the architectural feat built. She scoffed. "It's the slowest month of the year for tourists. Most of the people here during winter are living past the highway. Yeah, I think there will be plenty of room."

She peeked a look over his shoulder to read the speedometer. He was pushing her Bug as fast as it could go. Much longer up the hill at such speeds and her car would likely shake itself apart. It was too old to be pushed like this. She wasn't about to encourage him to take it slower, though. The rearview mirror glinted with a flash. Behind them was a silver Hummer approaching fast. "David!"

His knuckles turned white, his fingers gripped the steering wheel with such force. "I see. Get down. They're either rich tourists eager to get away from the tsunami or we've got unwelcome company."

Aria knew which of the two it was. There were no other resorts or homes behind them on this road other than the conference center. *Lord, please keep us safe from these men. Please help us get somewhere safe before the tsunami hits, and help everyone in its path get to an evacuation zone.*

The sound of a gunshot hit her ears. She strained to look in the side mirror. One of the thugs was standing up through the sunroof, aiming at them.

"Are you hurt?"

"No."

David's eyes darted from side to side. She knew he was trying to find a place to turn, to hide. Sadly there were only small businesses and a few vacation rentals along the way. There wasn't another road they could take that wouldn't lead them parallel to the ocean or back down to the shore. To their left was the state park on top of the cliffs, but there was no road to it besides the highway.

They needed to go straight east, away from the coast. And she was pretty sure George's murderers knew it too.

David fought the steering wheel for control. The Bug was still chugging forward but slowed ever so slightly. The sand dollar hanging from the rearview mirror swung in a pendulum arc from all the shaking. *Lord, help!* He needed to get out of the line of fire. *I just need more time. Please hold off the waves.*

The road widened, and the Hummer sped past them. The gunman turned around, his torso just above the vehicle's roof, until he faced them. This time the car didn't obey David. "We've been hit!" The Bug spun sideways, and another gunshot jolted the car. "They're trying to leave us here."

"If we don't get to the evacuation zone before the tsunami hits, we won't get out. You can't outrun—"

"I know," David interrupted. He didn't need to be reminded that if the gunmen didn't kill them first, the tsunami would. His throat burned. A metallic shine to his left caught his attention. He jerked the wheel and slid them into a cracked open aluminum shed—as if the occupants had left in a hurry—and prayed if the Hummer came after them, they'd pass it by as inconsequential. The Bug barely squeezed into the space without hitting the ATV in front of them. "Never thought I'd be thankful for this car's small size," he muttered.

He prayed the all-terrain vehicle was in working

condition otherwise they'd have to flee on foot. David jumped out of the car. "Look for the key to the ATV."

As she stepped out of the car, he grabbed the string wrapped around the rearview mirror and tugged. The thread snapped easily in his hands. As he jogged around the front of the car, he slipped the preserved sand dollar into the front of his tool belt.

Aria threw her hands up. "No key in sight."

"I knew it would be a long shot." David straddled the seat of the purple-and-chrome four-wheeler. Never had he been so glad that he and his brother had been stranded in the mountains a couple of years ago, their key lost among the sea of sage bushes. With the help of his cell-phone browser and video tutorials, he had learned how to hotwire the ATV. David prayed this model worked the same way.

He fumbled for the pocketknife in his tool belt. He flipped open the flat blade and applied pressure to the area around the keyhole. Despite the sickening crunch of breaking plastic, he kept working at popping out the ignition, using the knife as a lever. He didn't care about keeping the four-wheeler in good condition and he doubted, at this point, the owners cared either, as long as they were somewhere safe. Everything in town was about to be underwater anyway.

The circular keyhole popped out, despite his trembling hands. He imagined this was how SWAT teams felt while defusing a bomb—in his case, the bomb being the tsunami that could destroy them at any moment. He pressed harder with the knife. He just needed the tabs to come off so he could get it going.

The parts he needed were now exposed. David

leaned over the side and tried to start it. Nothing. He heard a rumbling outside the shed.

"I think it's the Hummer coming back," Aria stated.

"Hop on, then."

She squeezed behind him. The four-wheeler may not have been meant for two people but they were going to have to make it work.

Aria jumped off the ATV.

It cranked, then died. His heart raced. He had almost gotten the ATV working. "I can't keep you safe if you're not going to stay with me!"

She spun around from the wall of the shed with two helmets, one in each hand. "Would be a shame if we escaped from the tsunami and the gunmen only to be killed by accident. You focus." She shoved the helmet onto David's head and attached the buckle for him with expert hands, although it was hard to keep working while looking over her wrists. He wanted to growl at her, but she had that determined look in her eyes. Best not to argue. A second later, she slipped behind him.

David squeezed the starter. *Lord, I really need this to work*. He cranked the handle and the engine sputtered to life. *Thank You*. He turned his head sideways. "Hold on to me tight and squeeze the seat with your legs."

It was going to be a bumpy ride. They needed to get vertical, and fast.

He revved the engine and they shot diagonally out of the shed's entrance, heading due north. Time was moving too fast. With the Hummer on the roads he doubted they could make it to the evacuation tower. And even if they did, then the people there would also be in danger from the gunmen. They needed to make it to the state park—and get there a way the Hummer couldn't follow. If they could make it to the bluff, they'd be out of danger from the tsunami, and hopefully from the men...at least for a while.

He heard another engine fast approaching. A quick glance over his shoulder confirmed the Hummer had pulled up right behind him. It was time to see how fast the four-wheeler could go. He searched for gauges— no fuel gauge, no speed gauge. He would have to push it for all it was worth and hope it had enough gas to get them to safety.

A firecracker sound hit his ears at the same time a sharp corner dug deep into his right rib. He shouted and arched his back but somehow he was able to keep his hands on the handles.

"They shot my computer," Aria cried. "The battery saved you!"

The sharp pain dissipated but a dull ache remained. It was the corner of her laptop that had shoved underneath his rib. Her computer? He hadn't been shot?

To his left, only a sliver of sun over the ocean remained. David swerved to the right at the sight of a dirt mound in the distance. "Hold on," he shouted. At full speed, he aimed directly at the middle of the mound. It was the closest thing to a ramp he could find. He just hoped it'd be enough to jump over the creek.

Her arms clutched around his waist a half second before the vehicle went airborne.

SEVEN

David squeezed the seat with his legs and hoped Aria was doing the same lest they separate from the machine in midlaunch.

He braced himself, but the impact still jarred his bones. He pressed the throttle down. The four-wheeler spun to the right, where the ground started to weave up to the top of the cliffs among black boulders. Aria's grip loosened, and he feared he'd lost her until he felt her nails dig into his side. He tightened his stomach but wasn't able to handle the sting much longer. "Your nails," he yelled.

Her hands slid around and latched in front of his stomach just as he had to whip the handle around to avoid another boulder. They were making their own path as the sun dipped below the horizon. He zigzagged left and right over and over again at full speed. The sand and dust kicked up, and David was suddenly more than thankful that Aria had insisted on helmets. While the sand stung his neck and the dusty air filled his mouth with grit, he could still see.

He couldn't afford to look behind him to see if the Hummer was still in pursuit. He jerked the handles to the left, barely able to stay upright inside another hairpin turn as they ascended a hill never designed for hikers or vehicles. Aria was having a tough time breathing, judging by the way her shoulders rose and fell against his back.

Ahead, the hill split into two different mounds, but David prepared himself for another sharp maneuver. They needed to take the most vertical route.

"Look what's coming," Aria screamed.

"I can't! I know they're shooting at us."

"No. The sea. It's being sucked back." Her voice shook and her arms squeezed tighter around his middle.

He understood from growing up near the coast that if the sea ever retreated backward at an alarming rate, then you'd better run because it meant a tsunami was imminent. Unfortunately, in such an instance, most people saw fish flopping on the beach and ran toward the ocean as if it was a sudden low-tide treat. Thankfully, because of the bad weather, there didn't seem to be any uneducated tourists in danger. Because once a tsunami started, the ocean could roll in at speeds up to five hundred miles per hour. There was no outrunning or outdriving a tidal wave.

David dared to glance down. They were maybe twenty-five feet up, but the ocean wave could be as high as thirty feet, judging by the strength of the earthquake. It was still too close for comfort. The four-wheeler started to choke and sputter. "No!" *Lord, help us. We need to get higher!* The vehicle chugged along at a slower pace but kept climbing the sharp incline. His eyes rose to the sky, where twinkling stars grew brighter. *Just a little farther.*

"Can't you speed up?"

David clenched his teeth. "No," he hollered back. "Is the Hummer gone?"

"They drove away. They're close to the highway by now, I expect. But I think they can still see us, David. The whole town would be able to see us up here."

"Right now all I care about is a wall of water not being able to see us." He maneuvered the ATV forward and crested the last hill. He breathed a sigh of relief. They had to be over a hundred feet above shore now, hopefully even more. A brown sign in front of three Sitka trees warning hikers not to go farther let him know he was entering the state park. He'd let the rangers lecture him tomorrow for treading all over the plants. He wouldn't have blazed a new trail if it weren't necessary. They hit a rock he hadn't noticed in time to avoid. His chest slammed into the front of the handles.

Aria jumped off the back of the ATV and slipped on the slick plants and rocks. David reached out with his right hand and grabbed her wrist. Her back was an inch from the sharp edge of a small boulder. She pulled on his arm, her legs straining until she returned to an upright position.

He dismounted and put a hand on her shoulder. "We should be safe here."

They slipped off their helmets and hooked them on the handlebars. He dared a look in the direction of the highway. An outline of a dark, square vehicle sat on the top of the hill near the highway. The headlights shone in their direction.

"That's the edge of the safe zone," Aria commented. "If the evacuation map can be trusted, that is."

"They're watching us. Trying to figure out where we're going."

Aria groaned. "So they can follow us."

David's ears twitched at the sound of a massive incoming wave. His eyes adjusted to the twilight. The shadow of the ocean's approach shot fear straight to his heart.

Aria took an involuntary step back despite knowing the state park was considered an evacuation zone. Theoretically, they should be safe here. She'd read about tsunamis and heard the tales from some of the locals who had experienced it years ago but, she realized now, she could never have been prepared for the sight and sounds erupting below.

A gust blew her hair back, whether from the wind or the sheer force of the ocean approaching, she couldn't ascertain. It wasn't like anything she'd imagined. It didn't resemble a tidal wave. It was more as if the entire ocean decided to move and make Sand Dollar Shores part of the sea. And the water kept coming.

David's hand covered hers, but his hand was trembling as well. "Please let everyone be safe, Lord," he prayed aloud. "All along the coast. Please let them have listened to the warning and gotten to safety in time." His voice was strong but strained.

She moved toward him, terrified at the potential loss of life below. He wrapped his arms around her, and they clung to each other, not able to take their eyes off the scenery below. She was stunned and paralyzed at the sight. In that moment, it was as if they were the only two people left in the world, and the sudden loneliness was crushing.

The winds shifted direction and the clouds moved to make way for moonlight. Aria gasped. The buildings had at first seemed to withstand the ocean as the water slammed against them, but as if changing their mind, the structures broke off their foundations and joined the current. The sound of the wave was magnified two hundred times by the snapping of trees and buildings, as if they were made from rubber toothpicks. Aria's shivers magnified into violent shaking.

The debris moved as one, now resembling matchsticks and boxes. Cars rose up to the top of the water and swirled alongside them. The entire small town she'd come to love was destroyed. David squeezed her shoulders, but his arms shook and she knew the devastation had an effect on him as well.

This place had been her second home, and after her father died, it had become her only refuge from pain. Now it had vanished in the blink of an eye.

"I can't believe what I'm seeing," David said.

"Most people don't realize a single cubic yard of water weighs almost seventeen hundred pounds," she muttered.

In her peripheral vision she saw him turn toward her. "You memorized the warning pamphlet, didn't you?"

She shrugged. In many ways, she was a different person from the girl he once knew, but some things hadn't changed. "Guilty," she admitted. Her gaze moved to the tower set just below the highway as the waters rushed toward it. "Imagine if this much water had hit us at this speed." She trembled. It wasn't the water she worried about—she knew the architecture of the evacuation tower was sound, but like a tornado, the debris a tsunami carried with it at high speeds was the unknown variable.

"Please let it hold. Let it hold," she chanted. She squinted and witnessed the waters rush past the tower. The tower stood strong. "It didn't crumble," she cried aloud, laughing in relief.

"At least *they* didn't seem to have cut corners. It seems to be holding." He squeezed her tight. "I was so overwhelmed earlier that I never thanked you for what you did in that hallway. I hate that you could've been hurt, but you likely saved my life."

She looked up at him in surprise. The relief that they had been spared, as well as anyone who had made it to the safe zones, snapped her out of her shock. She was still in David's arms, his strong arms, and he was being nice. Despite the chill, her breath felt hot as it slipped past her lips.

"It's times like these you realize how precious life is," he continued.

Her heart agreed with him, no matter how clichéd the sentiment, but her mind screamed danger at the change in his demeanor. She stepped out of his embrace. "I don't see the Hummer anymore."

He didn't seem to mind her abrupt change in course, both in proximity and conversation. "Either they've driven away or they've turned their headlights off," David said. "I can't make out anything but dark shadows near the highway."

She tasted the salty air, but the sensation brought her no pleasure. The ocean had invaded. How long would it take before it went back to where it belonged? Was everyone spared? Anxiety tightened the muscles in her stomach. She needed information. She needed to feel connected with the rest of the world. But someone still had to bring about justice, to catch those men. Part of her hoped that the waters had reached George's murderers. Her throat burned with rage but also guilt for even thinking such thoughts.

"How long a drive until the Hummer gets to the state park?" David asked.

It was the mental slap she needed to refocus. "What do you mean?"

"Since we know they made it to the highway, how long of a drive would it take for them to get into the state park?"

Aria bit her lip. "Assuming they could go anywhere on the highway, ten or fifteen minutes?" She pictured her mental map of the highway. Directly to the east of the highway, past the houses dotting the foothills, was mountainous terrain. No roads led straight east. It was a dead end past the highest house. They weren't a big enough community to warrant other roads, making Highway 101 their only way out.

To the north was the town of Beachside, but she didn't know if the accident and car pileup the dispatcher had mentioned was to the north or south of the state park entrance, or if it had been cleared before the tsunami. If they hadn't, surely the police would've heeded the tsunami warning and made people carpool or run to get to safety in time.

The state park kept the highway farther back, but for the rest of the jagged coast, the highway ran precariously close to the beach, which meant the tsunami waters likely blocked their only way out.

Inside the state park, there were miles and miles of trails and paths. The main, and only paved, road wound all the way to the farthest ocean overlook, but she didn't know how long it would take the men in the Hummer to drive. "Thirty minutes to get to this point…at the very most," she concluded aloud, but knew it could be a lot faster.

"Get back on the four-wheeler then. We need to get somewhere safe to hide before those men find us."

EIGHT

Aria grabbed his wrist to keep him from starting the engine. "Wait a second. Let me think." It helped her memory if she closed her eyes. She hiked the park daily, weather permitting. The park took up most of the space on the elevated range but not all. Some prime real estate that bordered the park's forest to the east—yet still boasted an ocean view—had been filled with tall vacation homes. "There are some houses on the edges of the park."

"Good hiding places?"

"At least somewhere we can hide until the authorities can reach us."

David shook his head. "Sounds good, though I have a feeling we're the cops' last priority right now."

She released his wrist and put on her helmet before slipping behind him on the four-wheeler. The fear of being shot or wiped out by a ton of water had lessened enough that she became fully aware of the sensation her wet clothes stuck to her cold skin caused. She was soaked, in the winter, and running for her life while the rest of the coast suffered through a natural disaster. It was too much. She wanted to press into David again for comfort and warmth, but he was wet as well, not to mention she didn't want to give him the wrong idea.

Her mother's words came back to her. *He's just like your father.* It wasn't true in personality or looks but more in his stubbornness and choice of occupation. She'd seen her father fall at the construction site, and there was nothing she could've done to prevent it. The grief alone may not have been enough to run from a relationship with David, but seeing her mother left with a shell of her former self would've been if David hadn't ended it for her. She shared the same passionate zeal as her mother, and if her mother couldn't live life without her husband, Aria knew she'd be resigning herself to the same future if she chose to let her heart love David.

David revved the engine but sat still.

"What's wrong?" she hollered over the rumble. "Why aren't we moving?"

"I realized I don't know where I'm going."

Out of the couple of dozen houses on the outskirts of the park, Aria had often admired the blue house sitting on the east side. "Head southeast."

The moonlight disappeared again thanks to a large cloud. "I'd be glad to if I could find a trail. Our risk of running into a tree is higher with each passing minute."

The darkness intensified, but she had no other suggestions. At her silence, he shrugged and put the vehicle into motion, albeit slow motion. It puttered through the landscape, but without a trail they bounced over the plethora of rocks scattered among the vegetation. The ride jarred her spine as her head jerked left and right. The headlights dimmed. David swerved around a young spruce that seemed to appear out of nowhere. It was so close, her shoe scraped against the bark. A cold splattering of drizzle hit her face. Great. The weather was working against them.

A choking, guttural sound accompanied the shuddering of the vehicle. She clenched her jaw. "Please tell me that's not us."

The four-wheeler lurched forward, and she slammed into David's back again. He groaned, and she realized her helmet had hit him between his shoulder blades. It had to have hurt. The ATV lurched forward once more and sputtered to a stop.

David slapped the front fender then sagged over the handlebars. "I think it's out of gas."

"Great. This is great. The entire coastline is dealing with the effects of the tsunami and we're out of gas, in the rain, with two homicidal thugs after us." Her anger was in such full force she couldn't rein it in. She dismounted the ATV, picked up a rock and threw it as hard as she could into the black void. Her voice cracked. "I don't understand why God is letting all of this happen. Those men, George, the earthquake, the tsunami—"

Her throat closed tight. She wanted to mention every other thing in her life that she didn't understand—her father's death, her mother's withdrawal from life—but she'd already said too much. She tripped over another rock, and caught herself against one of the mammoth tree trunks. She turned around, took off her helmet and leaned up against the tree for support. A moment later his hands were on top of her shoulders. She didn't look up but heard David's sigh.

"I don't understand why either, Aria, but I figure

He's a big enough God to handle our questions. It's His job to know and our job to put one foot in front of another while we trust and obey Him. And hopefully, we'll get to know the answers we seek someday."

She felt her eyes widen. His words didn't sound like those of the immature guy she'd verbally sparred with earlier.

"I don't always live like I believe that," he said, as if he'd read her thoughts. "But when I realize that my actions don't match my beliefs, I just try to do the very next thing right."

She lifted her head. She didn't want to share her struggles with trusting the Lord right now. It hurt too much to admit and she wished she had kept her mouth shut in the first place. Aria inhaled and looked up into his face. "I appreciate you trying to comfort me, but I just want this to be over." The moonlight accentuated his strong jaw, his green eyes and his broad shoulders.

He stared at her for a moment before nodding. "Regardless, I need to focus on the very next step. We need to find shelter before those men find us. The ATV's out of commission, but we can't stay here. It's time to set out on foot. At least until help can reach us."

The heavy bag on her hip reminded her she still wanted to get her hands on the information on the flash drive. It's what George had wanted, and it was the least she could do to honor his last request. The moonlight disappeared, covered by clouds again. She fumbled for her phone and turned on the flashlight.

"No," David said. "There's no brightness setting on the flashlight. If they're out there it makes us easy targets. Let's put our screens on low brightness and use them the least amount possible."

She followed his suggestion but it meant only seeing a few feet in front of her. "How on earth are we going to find our way like this?"

A small movement in the corner of her vision took her breath away. Something brown and fluffy was moving. She swung the screen light in the direction. She exhaled. "It's one of the rabbits."

As if in answer, it bounded a few more leaps and turned to look back at her. It was standing right underneath... "A sign!" she cried.

"You beautiful, smart animal! Thank you." She ran up to the wooden state park trail guide, complete with yellow arrows, as the rabbit hopped away.

David shook his head. "Aria, you can't possibly believe the rabbit led you—"

She held up a hand. "Let me have this moment. Even if it's a delusion, it's a welcome one. I have my bearings, we have a trail and things are looking up."

David couldn't help but laugh. This was a glimmer of the Aria he remembered—the passionate, spontaneous, upbeat, light-hearted girl. It was good to know that even in the darkest of moments, this side of her still existed. The only problem was it made his heart soften, a dangerous side effect. He couldn't afford to let his affections for her grow again. "Which way do we go?" he asked.

Her fingers drifted over the letters. "The Spruce Wild Trail should lead us to the southern outcropping of vacationer homes. Most of them—if not all—should be empty right now."

David followed behind her, glad for their phones. But if they kept relying on them, their batteries would be dead within an hour or two, and without a charger, he didn't want to take that risk. The moment his feet reached the flattened dirt path, he switched his phone off.

Aria stiffened. "What is it?"

"Trying to save battery."

She huffed a sigh. "Well, talk to me before you do stuff like that."

David clenched his jaw. Was she seriously trying to give him a lesson on communication? Yet another reminder of that interaction two years ago—he had bared all of his feelings in that card and she responded by saying she needed space. David suppressed a growl. Embracing anger was better than allowing hurt to paralyze him again. Yet it was better to remain silent than open his mouth and say something he'd regret.

"David?" she asked. Her phone screen went dark. He stopped. "Yeah?"

"I'm sorry," she said softly. "I have no right to bark at you. It's an understatement to say I'm on edge and the phone going dark gave my heart a jolt. I thought you had spotted someone."

His heart softened as fast as her voice had and he changed the subject. "So, you're familiar with these trails? How far a walk we talking?"

The beam from her screen turned back on and he followed her quickened pace. "If we keep moving at a clip, I'm going to guess it'll be a good thirty minutes before we start seeing houses.

"Isn't that how much time you thought we had before the Hummer reached us?"

"Uh…yeah, but as you pointed out, we don't exactly have a lot of options. I'd run if it wasn't dark but as it is, I think it's too risky. Besides, do you hear my shoes? If I ran, the squeaking would be even worse. These things are soggy beyond belief."

"You're not going to like this, but I think if we're not there in fifteen minutes, the phone has to go off entirely. I don't want them having any way to track us."

The phone beam swung with her swinging arms. "Then you better pray the clouds move enough so we can see...but not enough that they can see us."

David looked up only to see blackness. Where had the stars gone? He squinted to make out the layers of odd shadows. "I don't think it's the clouds we need to worry about. We're covered underneath a canopy of tree branches." His stomach released a loud gurgle.

"Me too," Aria said.

He cocked his head in her direction. "I didn't say anything."

"Your stomach did, and I agreed. I'm hungry but I've never been this thirsty." Her teeth chattered. "I might be a little cold too."

A gust of wind rushed past the trees and through his hair. As if in reply, goose bumps covered his arms. He tried to block out his own discomfort by straining his vision. Focus proved to be a powerful ally. They walked in silence for a few minutes, and David's eyelids grew heavy. He stumbled over something—a rock? He bucked forward and pressed his hands onto his knees until he was steady.

"Are you okay?" Aria's hands were on his back, ready to offer him support.

He laughed. "I appreciate the gesture, but how did you think you were going to help me? If you tried to hold me up, you'd go down with me."

"Instinct," she responded. "At least you only tripped over a branch. There are sometimes full-sized fallen logs on the trail."

He straightened, his stomach and pride a bit bruised but otherwise intact. "Doesn't bode well for turning off the lights, does it?"

"I think we lose the tree covering around the bend." True to her word, the sky made an appearance and the wind whipped across his face. "Stay close to me, David. It's another overlook with a steep drop. The Gillamook viewing point."

He spotted the moon. It hung low to the east, just above the treetops up ahead. "It's almost a full moon."

"Perfect for lighting our way." Aria slipped her phone in her pocket. Her right shoulder hung down low from the weight of her bag. Wordlessly, he lifted the strap and took it. He remembered the photograph she had slipped into the bag before the earthquake. David couldn't help himself from asking. "Did you check to see if your picture was damaged?"

She lurched to a stop and spun toward him. "I hope not!" While he held the bag, she sunk her hand in and pulled out the frame for a moment. The moon reflected off the glass cover, but it was enough light to see her brilliant smile in the middle, with her mother and father on either side. Aria breathed a sigh heavy with relief and dropped it back in the bag. "It's not damaged."

David hesitated. He wasn't going to ask about the framed photograph but he also knew conversation was good to keep them focused. With the half-hour hike ahead of them, they needed safe topics. "How are your parents doing?" David asked. "Your dad still building away?"

She halted, her mouth dropped and her breath turned raspy and shallow. David reached a hand out. "Aria? Are you okay?" He fumbled for his phone. Had she been hit by something?

"My dad died." Her voice was low and gravelly. "You know that. You might not be happy with how things ended between us, but I never thought you'd be so cruel as to play mind games."

NINE

Any remaining adrenaline coursing through his veins dissipated. He sagged forward, his heart throbbing against his rib cage. Surely he had misheard. "Wh-what? Your dad died?"

"Don't pretend. Please."

Acid rose in his throat. He shook his head. "Aria, I promise. I had no idea."

She stepped forward, the moon highlighting the ways her eyes narrowed. "How could you not know?" Her eyes were wet. When she shook her head, a tear dropped.

"It's no game." David closed his eyes. "I didn't know." A man he had admired and respected, like George, also gone? They were examples of what he wanted to be as a man. It was too much. "I'm—I'm so sorry." His stomach burned. "When?"

She stepped back, uncertainty written on her face as she tilted her head. "He died a couple of years ago."

David's head dropped forward, his mouth agape. "A couple of years ago?" Aria remained silent, her arms wrapped around herself. David examined Aria now. She seemed far away, lost in thought. "Your dad was a great guy."

"Yes, he was. Thank you," Aria said, her forehead still crinkled in a frown.

David straightened and pressed through his foggy thoughts and tried to do the mental math. After he had reacted in hurt during their phone call and essentially ended their relationship, he had gone to visit a few days later to apologize in person only to find the house empty and the house for sale. His parents hadn't been able to reach them either, but David had assumed it was their wish to end to the relationship. Had he seen everything through the wrong lens or... "It happened right after we broke up?"

She huffed. "Uh...no. May 1," she answered in a monotone. "At the construction site."

David did the math. They had broken up May 7. It had taken four days of texting her, asking if she had received it, and then they had spoken on the phone on the seventh. He replayed the conversation in his head. "So when you said you needed space..." He groaned. His heart physically hurt, beating against his chest hard. How could he have jumped to conclusions so fast? His pride had truly been his fall. "You really did need time. My card was such a bad idea. I should've told you in person, I should've been there for you."

Aria flung her hands up. "See? How can you tell me you didn't know about my dad when all you seemed to care about was whether I got your stupid sympathy card or not?" She dropped her face into her hands. He took a step toward her, but she blocked him with an outstretched hand.

David thought he might be sick. "It wasn't a sympathy card," he said softly.

Her hands swiped rapidly at her cheeks, wiping tears away. "Wh-what?"

"It wasn't a sympathy card," he said, this time stronger. He exhaled. She must've thought he was the biggest jerk to send a sympathy card and then hound her about whether she had got it. "I take it you never read it?"

She rolled her eyes and turned away, her face betraying her exasperation. "Stacks of cards arrived, yours included. I'm sure they all said the same thing. *Sorry for your loss.*" She inhaled a staggered breath and peered at him from the side. "You really didn't know he died?" Her voice held a tinge of disbelief. "My mom let your parents know. They were on the call list." Her shoulders sagged. "That was her one job," she said, her voice low, "and she couldn't even do that. I should've known it'd be too hard for her." Aria blew out a long breath. "I wonder how many other people don't know…people who have moved away, ones we don't see often."

David grabbed her and pulled her into his arms, hugging her tight. "I had no idea, Aria, but when you said you had received my card and needed space, I thought you were, well, rejecting me." He gritted his teeth. "I have only my pride to blame. If I had just asked you more questions…"

She stepped out of his embrace, wiped the moisture off her cheeks with both hands then stared boldly into his eyes, her eyebrow raised. "David, if it wasn't a sympathy card, what exactly did it say that would make you so upset that I needed space?"

He studied her face so full of anger, despair and uncertainty. This wasn't the right time now, especially after the years apart. There was a lot of hurt to be healed. "I hope to tell you someday, but I don't think now is a good time."

She eyed him but nodded. They walked together side by side in silence for a few moments.

"How...how's your mom?" he asked.

Her lips pursed. "Devastated. The moment Dad died, she left the house and went to her sister's. Didn't come back once, not even to pack. Had movers pack it up and put it in storage by the end of the week. She didn't want a single memory in that house without my dad."

David kicked a rock out of the way. Aria got her passionate, impulsive side from her mother, but he didn't realize just how intense her mom could be.

He had been drilled over construction safety in school, and for good reason. Almost twenty percent of all worker fatalities happened in his field. The "fatal four" were electrocution, getting caught in between things, being struck by an object and falls. He cleared his throat. "How, uh, how did he die?" David asked.

"I was helping out Mom by bringing him lunch," she said, her voice soft. "I had just parked the car and looked up only to see him fall...from the fifth floor."

David's feet stopped moving. He imagined what that must have been like for Aria and wanted to pull her in close and wrap his arms around her. But he hadn't been there for her, and she'd made it clear by her body language that she wanted him to keep his distance.

She kept walking. He took long strides to match her pace. "Why didn't you tell me in person?"

She glanced at him but then focused on the path

in front of her. "I assumed you'd have known since our parents knew each other. I was in shock for a few days and didn't want to talk to anyone, and then…days turned into weeks." She sighed. "I suppose I have as much of the blame to shoulder for our misunderstanding. I'm sorry I didn't tell you, but it wasn't personal. I pretty much lost contact with everyone. Everyone except George, that is."

David's pulse throbbed in his neck. He warred between grief, shame and anger and didn't know which one to address. "You thought I'd abandoned you, so you gave up on me?"

"Well, I'm sorry," she bit out. "My dad had just died in front of me, and my mom completely checked out emotionally. We never returned to the house. Never, David." She turned to him and pointed her finger at his chest. "So if you're trying to lecture me on how I should've known better, you'll have to excuse me."

David pressed his lips in a firm line. The reality of the situation was starting to fully weigh on his shoulders. All the angst and rejection he had felt was for nothing. He had put all his hope in one stupid written note and had chosen that method of expression with a pat on the back, imagining her cherishing it and showing it to everyone throughout the years. He wanted to punch himself for being so prideful.

She sighed. "Besides, we had never committed to each other, had we? We had dated long-distance, with big gaps of time without calling each other, except for the regular 'what you doing?' text. Again, I'm sorry, David, but I didn't have the heart to keep any casual relationship going. After my dad died, I didn't have the energy for anything extra."

David almost didn't see the boulder in the middle of the trail. He stepped around it at the last second. She thought their relationship had been casual? Sure, he had never told her in person how he had felt, but his actions had to have spoken louder than words, didn't they? She had to have known deep down how he had felt. The daydreams they'd imagined of their lives together, that had to have meant something, right? Or had his pride blinded him in that area too? "I went to your house once to see you," he added. "It was empty, with a for-sale sign." The pain between his temples grew.

"Mom did that within a week of Dad being gone," she answered.

"That doesn't make sense to me," he replied, automatically.

"Since when does grief make sense?" she asked, her voice harsh.

"Is your mom okay now?"

"Pretty much the same as the day Dad passed," she answered.

"I wasn't there for you," David said, "but I would've liked to be."

Aria was silent. "Some people reach out to others in their grief, and some people withdraw. I guess I'm like my mother in that way."

"And yet, you're very different from your mother as well."

She came to a sudden stop. "What do you mean?"

"Don't get me wrong, you have a lot in common with her, but your mother would've never shoved the closet open on a gunman, or lit a flamethrower." He grinned, but hoped his next statement would provide her comfort. "That courage and bravery came from your dad's side."

Aria said nothing but started to walk again, seemingly deep in thought. The skies opened up with rain. David grabbed her hand, and they ran until they were back underneath the canopy of trees. Even then, a drizzle seeped through and kept them wet and chilled. Up ahead, David saw something flicker. Was it distant lightning or something worse?

"I think those are headlights," Aria said, confirming his fear. "We need to go off road. We can't be too far from the houses, though."

He grabbed her hand. "Phones off."

They were in pure darkness—the thick branches made a roof that concealed all of the sky—which had pros and cons. George's attackers wouldn't be able to see them easily, but they couldn't see much either. David started to lead her to the right.

"No." She tugged back on him. "If we go that direction and lose our way, there's a chance we could end up too close to the cliffs."

"Lead me, then." She squeezed his hand and pulled him gently to the left. They stepped slowly and methodically into the underbrush, weaving between trees, for what seemed like hours. "Aria, I haven't seen the headlights for quite some time. Maybe we should get back to the trail."

She sighed. "Okay. I think we're almost there anyway." She let go of his hand as if it was on fire the moment they stepped onto the hard-packed soil. They had come to a fork. "We take the right, and it should lead us away from the park to private property."

The trees thinned a bit, and the stars and moon provided just enough light to see the outline of several houses in the distance. David's heart sped up. Shelter out of the cold and rain sounded like the best gift in the world. He was physically and emotionally spent in every way and he was sure Aria would admit to feeling the same. Lights flickered again, sweeping from left to… "Down!"

He shoved Aria to the ground and rolled her back into the wooded area. He hoped there weren't any of those sharp black rocks bordering the path. Mercifully, his back landed on ferns. "Crawl," he whispered. "Headlights."

"We were so close to safety," Aria whispered, her voice thick. They maneuvered the terrain on their hands and knees until they reached a tree. It'd have to be far enough. "Lie down." He slid an arm protectively over her waist as the headlights swept past the tree that was shielding them.

TEN

Aria shifted on her back a little to relieve the pressure from something pointing into her side. A stick of some kind. She stared hard up into the sky, looking for the lights. She smelled a mixture of salt and moss and rain that usually soothed her but today just reminded her that she hadn't had anything to drink or eat for far too long. Her throat ached with the effort of holding back tears and running for her life. And she couldn't even begin to process what David had just told her. He really hadn't known? She thought she felt something crawl onto her calf. She kicked her right foot until the sensation stopped. "I hope we're not on top of poison ivy."

David shushed her. "They might have their windows down."

The leaves rustled, twinkles of moonlight seeping past them. Then the leaves started to move faster, as if more leaves were joining underneath, and they were dipping down lower all at once. Aria's hands covered her mouth. A flapping sound accompanied by what sounded like mice squeaking and kids giving loud kisses filled the area. Bats. She cringed, and if not for

David's arm firmly holding her down, she would've run. The sheer number of them seemed to make the greenery all around them shift from the air current that passed. She couldn't take it. She rolled into David's chest. And a moment later, the forest was still again.

"My concern about noise seemed to be a bit off base," he whispered. "I can't stand bats."

She echoed the sentiment but wasn't ready to remove her hands from her mouth. The headlights swept back toward their area. After a moment they moved past, presumably headed for where the bats came from. Aria propped herself up on her elbows.

"What are you doing?" he chided.

"What if it's help or authorities?" Aria challenged. "I need to at least peek." She craned her head and tried to make out the shape of the vehicle that had just passed. One thing was for sure. It wasn't a police cruiser. It was bigger. She couldn't tell if it was the boxy Hummer, but it wasn't likely to be help. She flopped back down on the ground.

"It's them?"

She nodded. "Probably."

They sat still for a few minutes. Aria kept slapping her arms. It may have just been wind or vegetation brushing up against her but she felt as if insects were biting. What good were bats if they didn't at least remove the mosquitoes?

"You're making me itch," David commented.

She huffed. "Then get me out of here."

He sat up. "Fair enough. They seem to have been gone for a while." He straightened and held out a hand. She accepted and pulled. In the darkness, her senses had heightened. The touch of David's callused hand made her recall memories of dates in the past where they had walked side by side. She could see his smile. He had always been the jokester, never serious, always about having fun and dreaming big. He seemed different now—more thoughtful—but perhaps she shouldn't make judgments while they were on the run for their lives.

She released his hand and made her way back to the trail. Ever conscious that the Hummer was likely driving in circles through every path the park had to offer, she quickened her pace. The path had widened enough to allow two cars instead of one. Within a minute, they were in front of a small bungalow. "Not this one," she whispered. "We can't pick the first house we come to. That's what they would expect. Follow me."

"And you're sure these are all empty?"

"The people who buy these kind of places are the type that have two homes. Usually one in the city. They don't like the rain and the cold in the winter, even if it's mild compared to, I don't know, Midwest standards. Besides, there's nothing open aside from Grumpy Lou's Café during the winter. Only the die-hard locals stay." Three more houses down, they arrived in front of a house she had always admired. In the daylight, it was a gorgeous shade of blue, like a blue-gray sky just before rainfall, but the white trim brightened the mood it conveyed. In the spring it was bordered with azaleas, and in the summer she always stopped to smell the many hydrangeas, daylilies and beach roses lining the front path. There were no flowers now in the winter, but she still imagined that an owner that worked to keep the front landscaping so gorgeous despite living in a forest must keep their house immaculate inside. Besides, she was a sucker for Cape Cod–style architecture. "Let's try this one."

"Looks good to me," David said. "Now let's get inside." He slid her bag off his shoulder and handed it to her before approaching the front door. He removed two objects from his tool belt. Despite the lack of light, she assumed they were thin screwdrivers, because surely he didn't own a pickpocket kit.

He leaned down on one knee. "Keep an eye out," he instructed and wrapped his hand around the doorknob.

"Since when do you know how to pick a lock?" she asked, her arms crossed over her chest.

"The same way I knew how to hotwire an ATV," he answered. "That's what you get when you have a houseful of boys."

She shook her head. How had his mother survived the trouble-making the McGuire boys had gotten themselves into growing up? She did as David asked and swept her gaze over the trees for any sign of trouble. Her ears strained at the sound of a cracking branch. Likely due to the rain and shifting of the earth from the earthquake but nevertheless her heart raced. She looked over her shoulder. "Any progress?"

"Not so far," he growled.

She studied the gravel lining the path to the front door. She searched for any sign of something out of place, like one of those novelty rocks designed to hide keys. "Have you checked around the door for a key? The frame? The fixtures? Are you on a welcome mat?"

He sighed. "Aria, the more you interrupt, the less likely I'm going to get this lock picked. If you want to look around, knock yourself out."

Her neck prickled at his tone. He was just as stubborn as ever, but it didn't bother her. He had three brothers and was used to being in an all-male environment. She'd grown up around men like that—her dad's employees and then later the men in the architecture program. They all became focused and irritated when things didn't go as planned. Aria knew enough not to take it personally. Her mom had made sure she had understood that from a young age. Come to think of it, even George had been extra grumpy the past week. She imagined the man's pride kept him from opening up without having all the answers yet, but if he had just told her what was going on maybe she could've helped...or maybe not. If she started down the road of what-ifs she'd be no good to anyone.

She pulled back her shoulders. It was not the time to let her emotions get the better of her. After one more search of the area, she abandoned her post and took David's suggestion. A quick look around the porch got her nowhere. No doormat, no container, no key on top of the doorframe...

"Satisfied?" David asked.

She shifted her weight and put her hands on her hips. "Don't get cocky. I'm only trying to help speed things along."

"Sorry. But you can help by keeping a watch-out."

She stepped back off the porch. Maybe there was another way inside. She walked around the side of the house and stopped at the sight of a mammoth-sized square humming next to the air conditioning unit. She peeked around the corner. Still no headlights on the way. She hustled back to the hunk of metal and pointed her phone light in its direction. She noticed there was still no network signal on her screen, but then the light hit the make and model of the box. "An emergency generator," she murmured, with a smile. Not just any generator…the kind that cost over ten thousand dollars. Did she know how to pick a hiding place, or what?

More determined than ever, she kept one hand on the siding as she made her way to the back. With each step she let her foot test the terrain before pressing her weight down. The house was placed diagonally against the edge of the cliff for the best view, but given the earthquake and the tsunami, she knew the chance of mudslides had increased, and she didn't know how sound the ground was below her feet.

Aria kept a hand on the house until her fingers caressed smooth glass. She smiled and, using both hands, dropped them to waist level and felt around until she found it: a doorknob. A glass back door that likely had no dead bolt meant easy access. Her mom once had been locked out and when she had called for Dad to come unlock the door, Dad had suggested she try the old credit card trick on the door inside the garage, and it had worked.

Aria jiggled the knob. It was at least worth a try.

Slipping her hand into her bag, against the warped laptop, she found the small zippered compartment. Inside was her wallet. She pulled out one card at a time, and while not able to see what each card was, she could feel for the telltale raised numbers and know whether it was a credit card or a loyalty card. She chose one of the grocery store loyalty cards—in case she ruined it, she didn't want it to be important—and slipped it in the side of the door. She slid it downward while turning the doorknob with the right hand. It popped and released, swinging outward. She smiled. She was in, but David was still out front and in the open without a lookout.

Aria relocked the back door, accessed the flashlight feature on her phone and navigated around the living room furniture, through the dining room and around the hallway table until she reached the front door. She flicked the dead bolt and swung the door inside. David toppled over onto the wooden entryway.

She flung a hand over her mouth, trying not to laugh. "Sorry. Probably should've warned you."

"How'd you get in?"

Her eyes drifted through the trees. Flickers of light. Her gut churned. "Get in," she croaked.

He rolled in, and she closed the door, trying not to slam it. "I hope they didn't see the light from my phone," she whispered, her back against the door. Even though she knew logically they couldn't hear her, fear tightened her throat.

Aria sank down to the floor, lest she get caught in the light's beam through the decorative window shapes at eye level. David grabbed her hand. "Lord, thank You for this shelter tonight. Grant us protection and rest until help can arrive. Amen." His voice was strong, not shaken or quiet as hers had been. Peace seemed to pour over her head and run down her spine like rain, and she marveled at how fast his prayer had calmed her.

She took a deep breath and slowly blew it out. He squeezed her hand and released it, and she was bothered by how she didn't want him to let go. David stood and pressed his form against the closest wall. He sidestepped and looked through the tall glass window. "They're gone."

Aria nodded but wasn't ready to move. Sitting down and being still had allowed the cold to seep into her bones. Then the shaking began.

David reached for her. "You're freezing," he said, his teeth chattering.

She laughed, but her mouth was vibrating so much it sounded like a machine gun firing. "Well, you are, too. And I just tried to call the police again. The circuits are still busy. David, we're going to freeze to death if we don't find some dry clothes in one of these bedrooms that can fit us."

"I'd settle for a blanket and a clothes dryer, but I doubt they have on electricity."

"Most people do keep the electricity on in their second homes during the winter, with their heater on the lowest setting, otherwise they get mildew and mold. I doubt they left the gas and the water on, though."

"Hate to break it to you, but after the tsunami, I doubt we have electricity. Any chance they'd have a generator?"

"Living here? Better than just a chance." She grinned and told him the make and model.

He whistled. "That's the Cadillac of generators. That puppy can even handle running the furnace."

She beamed, so anxious to get warm and dry.

David reached up and flipped the dead bolt. "Let's hope we're safe here until help comes."

ELEVEN

Fifteen minutes later, David walked out of the bathroom, strutting like a new man. He was glad he could use his phone to light the way without fear of being spotted. Although they had electricity thanks to the expertly installed generator, he didn't want to risk drawing attention to the house.

Dressed now in jeans that were too big for him, a belt cinched to the last hole, a thick long-john shirt with a black Henley on top and wool socks for his feet, he found warmth was returning to his bones. He stepped softly down the wooden stairs, carrying his shoes in one hand in case they needed to leave on short notice. They needed to stay on alert in case of unexpected visitors. Aria didn't seem to have the same hesitations, though, as he heard cabinet doors slam shut. He stopped at the programmable thermostat and increased the temperature, temporarily. He'd never wished so badly to be clean, but since they weren't able to take showers due to the lack of water, the least they could do was get more heat running throughout the house.

He found Aria in the stainless-steel kitchen, her

phone propped on the counter, the flashlight setting illuminating half of the room. She straightened at the sight of him and gave him a once-over. He grinned and puffed out his chest for her appraisal. She gave a cursory grin and turned back to the cabinets, effectively deflating his ego.

No matter how he may have looked, she appeared graceful despite her quick movements fluttering about the kitchen. The white sweater and brown corduroy pants were too big on her as well, but still suited her. She'd even replaced her soggy tennis shoes with brown loafers. It was the type of outfit he imagined she'd wear on a relaxing day by a fire. He wished they could sit on the couch and dream about their futures like the good ole days but the murderers on the hunt for them stole his desires.

David examined the living room behind the kitchen counter. The vaulted ceiling led to the wall of windows, framed vertically and horizontally by rustic wooden beams. One of the rectangles within the frame was the back door he assumed Aria had used, and in the center of the room was a white sectional couch. Without a television or fire, it seemed the purpose was to relax and enjoy the amazing view the windows no doubt framed on a normal day—a day without destruction. The moonlight spread through the top two rows of windows closest to the ceiling.

"I don't think it's a good idea to stay in here. These windows make you an easy target."

"Then help me," she said.

"Say the word."

She stepped in a circle between the kitchen island

and the oven, her hands open. "Where would you put an emergency kit in a house like this?"

He frowned. "Assuming they even have one, why do we need an emergency kit?"

"Bottled water, a radio, some food…all these would be very welcome right now." She sighed. "If I go too long without eating, I get sick, and I'm so thirsty."

"As in hypoglycemia?"

"I'm not sure. I just know it's not good, and I'd prefer to be on top of my game instead of throwing up if we have to wait much longer for the police."

"You should really get that checked out."

"I'll keep that in mind," she said in a monotone, clearly annoyed he even suggested it.

"Have you tried the pantry?"

She nodded. "Already checked. Mostly pots and pans with some baking staples."

"Anything in the freezer?"

"No, the refrigerator is unplugged."

"Garage?"

She shook her head. "No, but that's an idea."

He turned on his heel then looked back at her. "Aria coming?"

She froze and let out a giant exaggerated sigh but looked as if she was fighting a smile. "Wow. I can't believe you went there."

"Why? Aria annoyed?" he asked again, wiggling his eyebrows.

She scoffed, but giggled and shoved him in the direction of the garage. "And here I thought I had left that old bit behind. Do you know that after junior high you were the only one that ever played that gag on me?"

He raised his chin. "Just doing my part to lighten the tension."

They opened the heavy door to the garage, taking care to check that it was unlocked before letting it close behind them. He flipped on his own flashlight setting on his phone. "My battery isn't going to last very long at this rate. We could turn the light on but there'd be a risk of someone seeing. I don't know how tightly sealed the garage door is."

She sighed. "We need to find a flashlight or something then."

"I agree, and I wanted to look over the garage anyway for possible weapons."

"You still the best nail gun shooter in the West?"

He chuckled, half-pleased she remembered, half-embarrassed. "Well, I haven't had any contest lately. Aside from my youngest brother, everyone's moved away."

David squinted and approached what he had prayed for…a workbench. Cables, wires and miscellaneous tools were spread out over the surface. There was a small red toolbox that seemed to also contain a jumble of tools within it, but no nail gun or staple gun in sight. What a disappointment.

Aria disappeared behind a stack of plastic containers labeled with black marker, things like Summer Fun and Fourth of July.

"Found it," Aria hollered. She emerged, an errant lock of curls sticking straight up. She held a plastic box labeled Emergency Kit high in the air as if she had discovered buried treasure. She strutted toward him. "I knew they'd have one. You'd have to be nutty not to be prepared when living on the coast. You never know when the power is going to go out."

She cocked her head. "Aren't you curious what's in here?"

He smiled and tentatively reached out a hand to smooth down her hair and winced.

Her smile dropped. "Your shoulder?"

He followed her phone's beam of light. A small red circle was forming on his shirt. "I guess the wound reopened. Stupid rock."

"That was no ordinary rock. It was big and jagged— but still better that than a bullet wound." She set down the tub. "I should've checked it as soon as we got somewhere safe. Can you slide your arm out?" She leaned down onto one knee and popped off the lid of the kit. "If there aren't any bandages in here, there's got to be some in the house, the bathroom maybe."

David slipped his arm out of the sleeve and pulled up the fabric just enough to see the wound. It was deeper than he thought.

She lifted out a black flashlight and an LED lantern. "Oh, I really hope it has decent batteries in it."

David heard a click and was suddenly bathed in light. He checked his phone—still no network—then turned it fully off and shoved it into his pocket. "We should take turns keeping our phones on in case we get a signal. I just turned mine off. Hardly any battery left."

"I'm still hoping we can find some chargers around the house. Water," she exclaimed. She pitched David a bottle and before he could even open it, she'd half guzzled hers. With a big sigh, she said, "Much better."

Aria set down the bottle, then thrust two cans of soup into the air while sporting an infectious smile. "Yes! Dinner and a first-aid kit."

She dropped the soup cans back in the tub and stood with the red canvas bag in her hands. "There's bound to be some bandages and antiseptic in here." She smirked. "Aria going to come closer?"

He chuckled. "Well played." He turned his shoulder to her and watched her face fall.

"This looks like it needs stitches, David."

He shrugged. "Not really an option now, is it? I've heard some of the crew talk about using duct tape instead."

She rolled her eyes. "Yeah, I've heard that, too. My mom and dad used to argue about that all the time." She cradled the bag with one hand and unzipped it with the other. "In third grade I had my first chance to use a straight-edge to help open boxes. Slit my finger right open. I thought my mom was going to have a coronary when Dad tried to use duct tape. In the end, she won. Emergency room and five stitches, thank you very much. Aha!" She grinned. "No duct tape for you today, I'm afraid." She pointed at the sawhorse leaning against the side of the garage. "Sit there."

He complied, so she set the bag down beside him. She held the lantern up to his arm and he turned away.

"Okay. Take a deep breath and when I count to three, blow."

"You think it's going to hurt that bad?"

"Do you want to bite your belt?"

His throat burned. Was she serious? He turned to her—ready to insist they use soap and water alone—

when he saw her twinkling eyes. "You're messing with me."

She shrugged. "It says it's no-sting antiseptic, but I'm not making any promises."

David clenched his jaw and prepared for the worst.

TWELVE

Even though Aria tried to make light of it, David's shoulder gash was quite large. She could see it had tried to scab over, but driving an ATV and running through the state park hadn't done him any favors. She squirted a healthy amount of antiseptic onto a square of gauze and took a deep breath for herself then pressed.

"You doing okay?" she asked, purposefully trying to keep her voice chipper.

"They lied," he grimaced.

"But you're all right? Not feeling faint?"

"Okay, maybe they didn't lie, technically speaking. It doesn't sting, it burns," he hissed.

She bit her lip and while keeping one hand on his shoulder, she prepped the largest butterfly bandage she could find. She hoped it would hold his skin together long enough to speed the healing, but there'd still be a risk of the wound reopening unless they got him to a doctor soon. "At least you weren't shot," she muttered.

"There's that," he answered.

"I'm afraid you might be left with quite the scar."

"Wouldn't be the first one," he answered.

His words triggered the memory of the first time they'd met. Not being one to enjoy sunbathing—she could never tan—she'd wanted to try her hand at stunt kiting on the beach. After all, the small town hosted a kite festival twice a year because the winds were so ideal.

So she had bought her first, and last, dual-line stunt kite. It was a lovely teal-and-black, and the shop owner offered to give her a tutorial. Foolishly, she had assumed the man was trying to hit on her and passed on the lesson. Because anyone could fly a kite, right?

Out on the beach, it became evident the differences between a recreational kite and a stunt kite. The slightest pull on either of the handles sent the kite into a dive bomb. She had been so thankful to be on a stretch of coast alone so she wouldn't embarrass herself while she tried to beat the spinning, diving kite into submission. Except the kite didn't want to be manhandled, it wanted to be finessed, but she grew impatient and frustrated. Aria hadn't heard a young man jogging, approaching from behind, until he had attempted to pass. Her kite dove straight for his temple. He crumpled to the ground, hollering. And that was how they had met.

Her fingers drifted to just above his ear. Underneath his hair she felt a long, jagged, raised bump. She cringed. "You still have it," she whispered.

He lifted his chin, his eyes searching her face. "Meeting you left a permanent impression." He glanced down at her hand. "Are you done?"

She inhaled sharply at the sudden heat growing in her chest. "Uh…yes, I'm done."

He grabbed her wrists. "Aria, in that card…well, I spelled out my feelings for you. I should've made a greater effort to seek you out. I let my pride be in charge. My ego was so fragile. It essentially kept us apart and, not only that, it prevented me from being there for you when you most needed someone. For that, I can only apologize and ask you to forgive me."

Her breath quickened and her throat became dry. She looked at his feet. "Only if you forgive me for withdrawing…for shutting you out without explanation."

She dared a glance back up at his face, and he nodded. She tried to smile.

"I'd like to start over," he said, his voice husky.

Her chest seized up, and she pulled her hands from his gentle hold, his fingers gliding past her palms and fingers. "David, I don't think that's a good idea." She stared into the light the lantern offered, searching for something that would make her focus, make her feel brave. "You have a career now but I…I'm back in school again. It'll be months before there'll be any work here after the tsunami, and even then, not the type of work you'd want. So it'd be another long-distance relationship—which I never want to do again—and aside from that, I don't think I can be with someone who works in construction. Not after—well, anyway, I could never ask you to leave your dream behind for me. So I think it's for the best if we just leave things as they are. As friends."

She chanced a glance at him. His lips were pressed firmly in a straight line. He nodded. "Friends?"

"I think it's better that way," she said so softly it came as a whisper.

He raised his eyebrows. "I make a pretty irresistible friend."

She huffed a laugh, not sure what to make of how easily he took her proclamation. She should've been relieved but the lump in her throat wouldn't leave. "I appreciate the warning," she tried to quip back.

Aria walked away, back to the cans of soup, shaken. The only way to avoid more grief was to get out of this situation as fast as possible. Her heart couldn't take any more for one day, so best not to let it feel anything.

"We need to keep a list," she said, trying to ease the awkwardness.

"A list?"

"Of…of all the things we use. So we can reimburse the owners."

David chuckled. "Even in the worst of times, you're thinking of others."

"Right now, the only thing I'm thinking about is food. I have to eat." She rifled through the tub. "What else do we have here…? Candles, matches, pop…"

"Pop? Who puts a two liter of soda in an emergency kit?"

She chuckled. "Someone who's afraid they might be without caffeine?"

He turned around. "I think I need to take stock of what else might be in here."

"Sure. You mind doing that while I heat up dinner?"

"How do you propose heating it? The microwave will produce too much light."

"Right. Stove then."

He shook his head. "I'm coming with you. I'll keep watch while you cook."

Aria frowned and almost refused him until she realized why. "The wall of windows," she acknowledged with a nod. "Okay. Thanks."

They walked to the kitchen in silence and made short work of finding a pot. She emptied the two cans of beef vegetable soup and cranked the heat to high—the faster, the better. Soup had never smelled so good. While she waited for the stovetop to heat up, she investigated the rest of the cabinets until she found a drawer with pens and notepads. She placed one of each on the counter and wrote, "Due to life-threatening circumstances, we were forced to seek refuge in this house. We had to borrow some of your clothes but will return them immediately. In addition, we owe you two cans of soup from your emergency kit and..."

Aria looked up. "Think we'll drink the soda?"

He squinted and bent over to read what she had written so far. Deep laughter bubbled out from him and she couldn't help but smile along with him. "What? What's so funny?"

"You! I thought you were teasing about leaving a list. I would've just left some money. With the tsunami, I'm sure the owners would understand even if we didn't have gunmen trying to kill us."

"Well, I wasn't teasing, Mr. Do the Next Right Thing, and the moment we get word of help coming or the roads being clear, we're not going to want to take the time to write a letter. Better now while I'm thinking of it." She tapped the pen in rhythm against the notebook. "We should probably leave them money instead of replacing the soup." She pursed her lips and debated what else to write. "I'm going to say we used the soda. We might need the caffeine later."

David shook his head with a grin. "How can you possibly be so thoughtful about the little things but miss the big things?"

A surge of nausea caused Aria to grip the edge of the counter for a moment until it passed. She hoped it was triggered by her blood sugar and not David's weighted words. Her cheeks burned with the heat. David had taken over stirring the pot of soup. She busied herself by finishing the note to the homeowners with the final words, "…and by the way, please consider installing a dead bolt on your back door for better security."

"Dinner is served," David said. Aria dropped the pen and turned around to find the soup already in bowls.

She accepted the steaming soup with two hands. "Where do you want to eat this?"

He shrugged. "I think there might be a home office with no windows behind the stairway. It's probably the safest option."

"An office? Do they have a computer?"

"Maybe," he replied with a shrug.

She was itching to find out what was on the flash drive. She steadied the soup in one hand and grabbed her bag off the floor. "Lead the way."

They stepped around the staircase and into the hallway. The light coming in from the wall of windows enabled her to see his dark form in front of her. She'd never been so thankful for a full moon.

"I need to close the door before I can flip on the light," he said. "Go in front of me."

The smell of books and cedar complemented the salty beef broth aroma as the click behind her draped complete darkness over them. With the sound of a switch being flipped, bright light flooded the room. She shut her eyes, waited a moment, blinked a few

times—until the stinging pain in her temples lessened—and looked around with a smile. The walls were
made entirely of bookshelves—filled with ancient en-
cyclopedias and other assortments of books. The floor
was covered with white carpet so thick she was sure
if she kicked off her shoes, walking on it would feel
like a foot massage.

"I love this room," she said. In the corner sat two
leather recliners, a round table positioned between
them. In another time and another set of circumstances, she'd have wished to spend a week in this
very room alone, devouring the books. For now, she'd
just savor the short reprieve and some dinner. The key
was to keep her mind off George, his murderers and
the destruction the tsunami had caused.

She set her bowl down on the table and dropped
the bag. It was the first time she could look at her laptop in decent light. She pulled it out and groaned. The
metal around the battery was bent back, almost as if
the battery had exploded into the laptop.

David slid it out of her hands. "So this battery is
who I have to thank for taking a bullet for me." He
glanced at Aria.

Aria shrugged. "I'm just glad the rumors about
these batteries turned out to be true. If I had a newer
model, the bullet would've gone right through. I can
handle treating flesh wounds, but I don't know what I
would have done had you been shot." It was true, but
she was also surprised at the emotional reaction she
was having about the possibility that David could've
been shot and the fact her computer was ruined. She
supposed since it was the last gift her father had given
her, it meant more than a laptop should mean to a per-

son. The mere thought reminded her of George and all the people stranded on the coast right now. She had no right to be shallow. She blinked away the sudden moisture. Since distraction wasn't working, she needed to find out what was on the drive George had wanted her to access.

She approached the desk in the middle of the room. The technology was ancient by current standards, but it seemed to be a working desktop tower connected to a monitor, mouse, keyboard and inkjet printer. "Please let it have a USB input." The keyboard didn't, but she kneeled down on the ground, looked on the back of the tower and found an unoccupied slot. "There's hope," she said, and returned to the chair to finish her dinner.

Aria took a tentative sip of the creamy soup from her spoon. "Not too hot, not too cold," she murmured. The warmth spread from her throat immediately to her belly, and a sudden exhaustion made her shoulders sag and her eyes droop. "I've never felt so weary," she muttered. "There's a verse in Matthew that says, 'For my yoke is easy, and my burden is light.' I've got to say this doesn't feel light."

David looked up, spoon in hand. He cocked his head and stared at her for a moment. "Galatians also says we should practice bearing one another's burdens since that's the law of Christ. I'm here, Aria. You don't have to carry this alone."

She released an exasperated sigh. "See, there you go, being all logical again."

He grinned. "Simply trying to give you a little more balanced perspective." David turned his gaze to the bowl and swirled his spoon around. "I was taught that if you studied the scriptures you'd find verses that didn't contradict each other, but rather provided balance, so that you would grow in the Lord like a tree does, with anchors on all sides to help you grow straight and balanced."

She took another sip, avoiding the barley swimming around, and processed his words. "I actually like that sentiment." They continued to eat in silence for a few minutes. Her bowl was empty in record time. She dropped the spoon into it and leaned back and sighed.

"Feel better?" David asked, his eyes searching her.

"Yes. The food helped a lot." She yawned and stretched her arms. "But I'm desperate to figure out why they killed George. I want to be able to tell the authorities who they are the minute they reach us."

She approached the computer tower, pressed the power button and waited for several minutes. After what seemed like forever a screen prompt asked for a username/password combination. She groaned. "Why can't it ever be simple?"

"So no success, then?" David commented.

Her fingers flew over the keyboard, accessing the DOS. The screen flipped to black as she typed in commands in the yellow, ancient-looking font.

"What are you doing?" David asked incredulously. He left his chair and stood behind her, watching over her shoulder.

"Trying something I learned in class."

"Since when are they teaching architects how to hack computers?" He took a seat on the desk, next to the monitor, so that he was facing her.

"It's ethical hacking, and they teach it to computer science majors," she answered simply. "Which is what I'm going back to school for."

David slapped his hand on the desk and leaned forward, his eyes bulging. "You're what?"

"I'm a computer science major. I went back to school this year, switched tracks," she replied. Why was he getting so worked up? He wasn't the one with huge college loans.

"Aria, the last I knew you were in your fifth year… your last year of college. You only had one more year of internship before you could get licensed as a full-fledged architect. What do you mean you switched majors?"

She clenched her jaw. "I didn't want to be part of that world after my dad passed, and my mom supported my decision one-hundred percent."

David's jaw dropped and he leaned forward, his hands on his knees. "You gave it all up? You've got to be kidding me. Being an architect was your *dream*."

She lifted a finger and met his gaze head on, determined. "Correction. It was my *dad's* dream for me."

Her argument didn't faze David. "Of course. It was my dream for you, too. Because you *loved* it. Because you were good at it—amazing at it, quite frankly. And I would know, because I've worked with other architects. It's all you talked about. It's why we had such a…a…casual relationship, as you put it, for all those years. Aria, you were working your fingers to the bone to accomplish your dream, and so was I…mostly to keep up with you! How could you leave that all behind?" His mouth dropped, his eyebrows rose and he leaned back, seemingly struck with a new thought. "Did the school refuse to give you an extension when your dad died?"

Her spine tingled. No one else had been that upset

at her decision. She'd had a scholarship for most of her schooling up until the point she switched, but as her mom pointed out, most people graduated with at least some college debt and "better you know now than after you spend ten years in a career you hate."

Her mom had been relieved, in fact, that she wouldn't be talking about construction sites and designs anymore. Mom wanted nothing to do with that life anymore, and Aria felt the same. Except now, she wondered…if she had stuck with it maybe she could've helped George and prevented everything that had just happened. She blinked back the emotion. "No…no, they offered me time to finish my classes, but it was my decision."

David raked his hand through his hair. "I…I'm speechless."

She pursed her lips together. What gave him the right to make her feel guilty about her decisions, anyway? "Well, apparently not speechless enough. Care to let me focus?"

He raised his hands up in the air with a shake of his head. "Be my guest."

Her fingers flew over the keyboard for a few more minutes. Her effort was rewarded. "I can at least access the USB files, but that's about it."

A pop-up box showed the list of files on the USB and her mouth dropped. What had George found?

THIRTEEN

David stared at the woman he thought he knew so well. How could she let go of all those years of schooling and her dream to be an architect? Because her father died? He knew she was passionate, and sometimes impulsive, but this didn't make sense. He was certain it had something to do with the way her dad died, but she wasn't telling him everything.

The soup wasn't settling in his stomach well anymore. He blew out a breath of frustration, but she was tapping the mouse in rapid-fire motions, clearly shutting down any further conversation on the matter. That was fine, he'd wait…for now. He felt more freedom to ask questions now that she said she wanted to be friends. David was only half teasing when he said he made a good friend. He was determined to be the best friend she'd ever had, and the way he saw it, a stellar friend had a responsibility to point out when his friend was making a bad decision. True, he could've been more tactful, but given the circumstances, he thought he was due some grace.

Aria pressed a series of keys and all the files popped

open, resembling a game of solitaire. "David, look. What do you make of these?"

"Besides a jumble of boxes?" He slipped off the desk and lowered himself down to his knees to examine the screen better. There were several different documents open on the screen. Some were scanned letters to George, but others seemed to be invoices and contracts.

"Look at this contract," she said, tapping the screen. "If I'm reading it right, it takes away all control or input George would have had in the entire remodel process."

David put his finger on the screen. "In exchange for this company paying for all the expenses. It's some investment sort of thing." They both silently studied the document.

"So they are in charge of getting investors and remodeling the place in exchange for ten percent of the invested funds. The investors in turn receive a certain amount of days of lodging in the new and improved resort." Aria leaned back in the chair. "Is that what you get from reading this?"

David shrugged. "You have more experience with contracts like this than I do."

"So when George suspected they were using subpar materials and fired the foreman and brought you in…"

"He was violating the contract," David concluded.

She stared at the ceiling, her eyes sweeping from left to right.

David leaned over her and clicked on the mouse. "Let's not make judgments without reading this more fully." He popped up a saved email.

Mr. Swanson,

I am the owner of a resort in Tallahassee, Florida. Recently, I saw your resort advertised as an investment venture. I hope this email turns out to be needless but my conscience wouldn't rest until I passed on what happened to me.

A group of men sold me a service and advertised for investors—the advertisement is remarkably similar to the one I am seeing for your resort. In my case, these men handed me a check at the end of the remodel, stating they'd achieved significant savings in the remodel. Later I found this check was given to me in hopes of keeping me quiet when everything started to fall apart—in more ways than one. You see, while they left town with the remainder of the profits, investors started to show up telling me they were sold condo shares. This was never to be the intention. The resort is not set up this way. We also discovered they used subpar materials and engineering that wasn't up to code.

Since then, I've found other similar resorts in the same mess. Each time the group of men have different names, different companies. They have a very impressive reputation—as they had people in town that could vouch for them. I also called every number on their reference list. All lies, a group part of their network. Those phones were all disconnected after the men left town. The FBI told me this is a scam they're starting to see more frequently.

If this sounds similar to what you were sold, I encourage you to visit these "testimonials" in person, or find the phone numbers of the owners on your own. Don't use their reference sheet.

Again, I hope this is not your case.

They read the letter in silence.

"George would've only violated a contract if he thought the contract was illegal. I heard him yell at those men that he wouldn't allow them to bamboozle people. What people?"

David shrugged. "The investors?"

She straightened and slapped the keyboard. "If we had any signals on our phone I could access the internet and find out more about this company, but the fact that he got shot shortly after this email—"

He leaned over and examined some of the other opened documents. "I've heard about scams like this. They show investors condos and convince them to invest in remodels. Then they do shoddy work, take most of the money—not just ten percent—and move on. If this email is right, then the supposed savings money they give owners might be in hopes of framing the owners." He sighed. "The last scam I heard about they traced to Russian mafia. Was George in financial trouble?"

"No, no, I don't think so. When I first came to visit him after my dad…" She cleared her throat. "Well, George had just gotten remarried and I overheard his wife basically begging him to take her on a cruise. She said he could afford it. She was tired of seeing him dump his money into the center." Aria's eyes widened. "I don't see George getting himself into this kind of agreement unless…unless he was convinced by someone he trusted." Her gaze flew up to meet him, her mouth open. "Like his wife!"

"You really think his wife is behind this?"

"No! I mean…it's just I keep forgetting about her. But after reading this, if they killed George, won't they go after her as well? She probably knows too much, don't you think?"

He sighed. "How would I know? Check your phone again."

She tapped the screen of the phone with an intensity that wasn't necessary for use. "Nothing. It only beeps. Busy, busy, busy. These things are worthless in an emergency."

"If the tsunami hit the entire coast, there are probably millions of people trying to check on loved ones and others trying to coordinate rescue and recovery. The phone companies don't have the infrastructure for that kind of surge of activity."

"I know." She shook her head, her curls bouncing in different directions. "I'm just anxious to know what's going on in the world. I really want to find out if the highway is clear. Maybe we should make a run to get help if it's not covered in ocean water." She shook the phone in her fist. "Especially since we can't reach help to come to us."

"Let's try the old-school method. I'll get that radio you found from the garage." He pointed at the computer. "You'll need to turn that off though. We need to have complete darkness before I open this door… just in case."

Her eyes drooped with sadness and exhaustion. "I thought that finding out why they killed George would help me. Instead it just makes me feel all the more helpless. Do you mind if I stay here and wait for you to get the radio? It's much more comfortable in here than the garage."

"Of course." He waited a beat and watched her close her eyes. She looked spent, yet beautiful. He flicked the light off. Once the darkness returned, David slipped out into the hallway only to see a flash of light reflect off the framed artwork on the wall, ten inches from his nose. He froze, every muscle tensed. Was someone in the house, or was that a flashlight from outside, refracting through the wall of windows in the living room? And if it was light, was it friend or foe?

There was a possibility it was floodlights from boats or helicopters coming to help tsunami victims. He tried to come to a logical conclusion, but there were too many variables. The light flashed again and this time he could tell it was the diameter of a flashlight beam.

"David?" Aria called out, and he could hear her footsteps approaching. "While you're out there could you get—"

He dove for her and slipped his hand over her mouth. She made a squeak then tensed in his arms. "Stay still," he whispered. "We've got company."

David felt her nod against his hand. She wrapped her nails around his fingers and pulled his hand down. She rose on her tiptoes and cupped her hand around his ear. "Are they inside?"

Her whisper was breathy, most likely in an attempt to be quiet, but it was hard not to jerk away. It tickled. He shook his head. He wasn't sure if they were or weren't inside, but he didn't think they'd moved indoors. There were no sounds of footsteps or breathing, except their own.

Almost as if they wanted to prove him wrong, a loud click sounded from the back. It seemed as though someone had found the same method as Aria had to break into the house. His mind cataloged the best possible places to hide, but before he could act on any of them, Aria pulled on his arm and darted back into the office.

He almost called out her name. The office was one of the worst places to hide—there weren't many options and no exit except the hallway door they'd come through—until he realized why she'd returned. She yanked the flash drive from the back of the computer and tiptoed back to her bag. Ah, if they found those then the jig would be up.

He heard shoes shuffling on the wooden floor in the living room. There was no place to hide now, nowhere to go from here and no more time for options. He grabbed the bag from Aria and shuffled her to the wall behind the door. If they hid behind the desk or the chairs they would be too obvious against the white carpet. What kind of people installed white carpet anyway? Were they human? Didn't they ever spill?

David gently guided Aria closest to the hinge of the door. She seemed to understand as she flattened herself against the wall and slid as far as she could, but there still wasn't enough room for him. David wanted to open the door farther but couldn't recall if the door had squeaked or not when they opened it. He stretched his hand past Aria and pressed against the middle door hinge—a trick he knew from many years of playing hide-and-seek with his brothers—as he shifted the door open another two feet.

He dropped his arms to his sides. The bag slid to the carpet, the straps hanging from his fingertips, and he stepped into the space next to Aria. The only thing left to do was to remain quiet and pray the men didn't look too hard.

The footsteps grew louder. They were getting close. Through the slit between the hinge and the frame he spotted the outline of one of the men, his arm outstretched. David's heart sank. He was armed.

The man turned, and the shadow disappeared. A portion of the beam of light slid through the space between the hinges onto the back of the wood. It disappeared as quickly as it came, and David hoped they didn't spot them through the small crevice.

The door started moving toward his nose. David felt his eyes widen. He grabbed Aria's fingertips, and they simultaneously rose on their tiptoes and, while keeping their backs pressed against the wall, turned their faces toward each other to prevent the door from hitting them. She dropped his hand and gripped his shoulder instead for balance. If the door bounced back at all, it would be a dead giveaway to their position.

The office light flipped on, and Aria's eyes widened, her eyebrows high on her forehead. She mouthed two words, but David couldn't figure out what she was trying to say. She rolled her eyes and mouthed the words again, her mouth opening and closing in dramatic fashion. Understanding hit him in the chest. The bowls…they were still in the room. They had left them both on the table sitting between the two chairs in the corner. An obvious giveaway. David clenched his fists. Should he take a chance and make the first move? Surprise would be their only ally, their only chance if discovered.

"Hold up!" the other man shouted from a different room. The office light flipped off and the footsteps retreated.

"What is it?" the gunman asked, his tone indicating his annoyance. Aria dropped her hand from David's shoulder and they both lowered to a regular standing position. David relaxed his hands and moved his head side to side to relieve the tension that had built up in his neck. He debated running to the table and grabbing the bowls while the gunman was distracted, but he knew he didn't have the grace to pull it off without alerting the men. If only he had been the one closest to the hinge. Aria could've handled it.

"They were here," the man grunted. "Listen to this: 'Due to life threatening circumstances,'" the man read in what David assumed was his best female impersonation the note Aria had left on the counter.

His eyes adjusted once more to the darkness and he watched Aria cringe. The men knew. It was only a matter of time before they found them and David had no idea how he would defend them with guns at play and no weapon of his own.

"This girl's a piece of work. We need to find them now more than ever, because mark my words—as soon as the phones are back up, this little girl is going to spill it all. There's no negotiation with someone like this. Ridiculous."

"Let's keep searching, then. They're here some-where."

"Is your brain on? Were you listening? Why would she leave a note if they were still here? They ate, got clothes and kept moving. My guess is they're head-ing to the highway."

"But the highway is closed a mile in each direction."

"Exactly, but how would they know that? As soon as they find out, they'll hide again, which is why we've got to catch them before that happens. Come on. Turn your flashlight off. We don't know how long ago they left. We need to make sure we don't alert them."

David's mouth dropped open. Aria's note had saved them? Her constant need to take care of little details was entertaining at times but mostly drove him nuts. And now he owed his life to it? He shook his head and ground his teeth together to prevent laughing at Aria's broad grin and twinkling eyes. She would be insufferable.

They remained motionless for three more minutes, but the way he itched to stretch it felt more like three hours. After the door slammed, they still didn't move for another minute. Just to be sure.

David snuck out of the room and peeked around the corner to make sure the men weren't trying to lure them out of their hiding place. The living room was empty. It appeared the coast was clear. He stepped back into the office. "You okay?"

Aria let out a loud exhale, crossed her arms and nodded at him, her eyebrows wiggling up and down. "How about that thank-you letter, huh?"

"Yeah, yeah, don't get a big head," he teased.

"Don't worry."

David stared at the wall of bookshelves. "Next house I work on with built-in shelves, I'm going to insist they include a secret passageway."

"All houses should have at least one," Aria agreed. "When you do, I have some designs you can use... some, uh, old ones in storage."

Once again David wanted to confront her with the decision of leaving behind architecture, but instead he ground his teeth together. "That was too close, and you heard them... They have no plans to give up looking for us. So, the very next thing we do is figure out some way to arm ourselves. You see any evidence of a gun safe in the house?"

"Not that I've found."

"Then we're going to have to come up with something in the garage to improvise."

She bit her lip and tilted her head up toward the ceiling. "It's kind of off the wall, but the pop bottle..."

He curled his lip. "What about it?"

"If they have an air pump then maybe—"

He inhaled with understanding. At least he thought he understood. "Are you thinking what I'm thinking?"

"We build a homemade air gun?" she asked. "You are, after all, the fastest nail gun shooter in the West. Or so I'm told."

He grinned. "I like the way you think," he said, and turned on and headed for the garage.

"Oh, sure, *now* you like the way I think," she said, right on his heels. "Where was that guy when I was writing thank-you notes?"

He couldn't lose the goofy grin on his face. Why couldn't she see how perfect they were for each other? His smile faded. Maybe she did see, but if she didn't

FOURTEEN

Aria looked around the corner, steeled her nerves and darted into the kitchen to retrieve an empty pitcher and two glasses. They needed an empty soda bottle for the base of the air gun.

"Wait. What are you doing?" David called out. "What's in there?"

"We aren't going to waste the soda, are we? I could use a pick-me-up."

He shrugged. "Fine by me. I want to take stock and see if we even have what we need to make the nail gun."

They entered the garage and she flipped back on the lantern left on the work counter. Aria lifted the two-liter soda out of the emergency box and set it next to him. She twisted off the lid and the sound of fizz bubbling to the top surged her taste buds into overdrive. Once they each had eight ounces she poured the rest of the soda into the pitcher for potential refills later. "Okay. Drink up." She turned and toasted him. "Here's to finding…a bike valve?"

He nodded. "Yes, that's a must. Along with…a gauge, a hose, some piping, a connector…"

"And either an air compressor or…"

"I'll take a bike pump if I have to," David finished.

Aria frowned and looked around the garage with new eyes. She thought she spotted a bike hanging on the opposite wall behind some of the other storage boxes, but she couldn't tell without a brighter light. "Not to mention the nails," she added.

They both took a long drink of the soda. "That really is a lot of stuff, isn't it?" Aria asked. Her creativity worked best when she thought things through aloud. She wasn't so sure the first idea that popped in her head was a good one anymore. "Are you sure they don't already own a nail gun or a drill or any power tool we could convert for an emergency weapon?" She spun around. "I mean these owners seem to have nothing but the best. I see a workbench…"

"Help yourself," David commented. "More power to you, if you can find it. I don't see anything but some loose tools."

Aria looked over her shoulder. "Well, you would keep all of your tools out in the open, ready for use, but here…if there was anything valuable and you only lived here half the year…maybe used it as a vacation rental sometimes, you would want to make sure the expensive stuff would be locked up." She pointed to some of the cabinets below the counter. "You'd be worried about that mildew I was talking about. So you'd probably pack it away until spring."

She bent down and started opening cabinets. Paper towels, safety goggles, nails. She shook the box at David. He crossed his arms and nodded, but she knew in her gut she was getting closer. She tugged on the next handle, and it didn't budge. "David, this one is locked. Point the lantern at it."

He obliged and there it was…a keyhole. "Think you can try out those lock-picking skills you were bragging about earlier?"

He eyed her. "You don't secretly know how to pick locks as well, do you? Because if I sit here working on it for ten minutes and then you come along with one click and open it, I'm telling you now I'm going to be mad."

She put her hands on her hips. "Now does that sound like me?" Laughter bubbled up inside. He knew her so well. If she did have lock picking in her arsenal, that would be exactly what she would do. The tendency came from working side by side with her dad and his employees. She'd grown tired of men thinking she was incapable and, on her dad's advice, found it was best to play naive until she knew without a doubt she could do it faster than the man in question. The element of surprise was what earned her respect on the construction site, but alas, picking locks wasn't something her dad had taught her.

She sighed. The laughing, the teasing—it all felt so foreign. And for the briefest of moments when they were discussing how to come up with a makeshift weapon, it was as if her old self had returned, energized by the prospect of design and innovation. She turned her back to David and topped off her cup while he kneeled down to work. She watched the bubbles slowly disappear into the shadowed cup.

After withdrawing from her friends—including David—her decision to leave her old life behind seemed sound. Sound… "I forgot about the radio," she said. She strode across the garage to get it. It took a few moments before she found a station without static.

Authorities warn that subsequent tidal waves often occur after a tsunami of this magnitude. Residents should stay in evacuation zones until the all-clear has been given. Highway 101 is closed along much of the Oregon Coast—from Astoria to Tillamook—due to massive flooding. Red Cross stations are quickly...

Aria closed her eyes, and tried to force back the sudden despair. Highway 101 was to be their lifeline and it was closed. How would anyone be able to help them? Aria turned the volume down for a second. "Did you hear that?"

David groaned, "Sure did. Any way we could just go straight east by foot?"

"How good are you at rock climbing without gear? Because it's a sheer rock wall on the other side of the highway—at least directly across the highway from the park's entrance."

"Okay, never mind."

"I never thought my haven would become my prison."

"Which brings us back to here. Arming ourselves is of vital importance. Hey, would you come here and point the flashlight while I work?"

She moved to his side and as soon as she got in a comfortable position on the cement floor she pointed it at the keyhole. He glanced quickly at her. "You interested in what I'm doing?"

It would be a welcome distraction. She cleared her throat. "Sure."

"I don't have official lock-picking tools, but I'm using the bit wrench from my pocket knife," he said, shaking his left hand, "as a tension wrench while I'm trying to mimic the key and hit all the pins with this other four-in-one screwdriver. Obviously I'm using the thinnest one." His shoulders rose almost to his ears as he grunted then released. "I'm not as practiced as I used to be."

"No doubt you and your brothers made that a competition, too."

He chuckled. "Mom encouraged it. Anytime she bought candy for us, she'd lock it up and let us take turns to get it."

"Your mom's hilarious."

David took a deep breath and inserted the tools back in the lock. "Yeah, I suppose she is. She found pretty creative ways to keep us occupied."

"Did she ever worry about what you boys would do with the skills? They could be used for less noble reasons."

"Nah. She made it clear what would happen to us if we drifted off the straight and narrow." He glanced up at her. "You know my mom used to be a cop, right?"

"What?" She leaned forward. "Are you serious?"

"Completely. Made detective before she and Dad decided to start a family." He shook his head. "We used to tease her that she never gave up that job, she merely worked for free. We could never get a single thing past that woman."

Aria almost asked to hear more stories but also sensed her connection to him strengthening. She didn't want to make him think she'd changed her mind about their relationship. The moment of silence increased her anxiety. She fidgeted with the sweater, as it hung down to almost her thumbs. "Do you think we're wasting our time? Maybe we should give up and do our best at making an air gun."

He grinned, turned and stared into her eyes but didn't move his hands from the cabinet. A sudden click, and the cabinet was unlocked. He wiggled his eyebrows. The beam of her flashlight bounced off the whites of his teeth. "Now, who's the man?" he asked.

She couldn't help but snicker. "Oh, you are definitely the man."

"That's what I'm talking about," he added, bobbing his head. "Now let's see what's in…" He pulled the cabinet door wide and the light caught three plastic cases resembling miniature suitcases, stacked one on top of the other. "Yes! Drill…circular saw…nail gun!" He slapped a hand on her shoulder. Shivers ran down her spine and she couldn't reply as he continued to gush. "You're a genius, Aria!" He gasped. "And it's cordless."

He removed his hand and pulled out the case. "Let's get this baby charged." He grinned again. "I love these people."

A flare of heat grew in her core. They had dated three years, known each other five, not counting the two years they had been apart and he didn't once— not once—tell her he loved her yet he could spout off how he loved the owners at the drop of the hat? She blinked the thought away. It didn't matter. He was just kidding around.

Her eyes drifted to a small silver box attached to the wall above David's head. He sobered and turned around. "What? A junction box?"

She nodded and approached the workbench. "I need a screwdriver." Her hands gripped the handle and she made short work of the screws holding the cover on top of the electrical junction box.

"May I ask what is so interesting about this box?"

Aria jumped a little at his voice so near. She hadn't heard him approach. His head was almost directly over her shoulder.

"One second." She popped it open. "There's plenty of room in here to hide the thumb drive." She slid the drive out of her pocket and placed it in the corner of the box where there was no chance it would touch the wires curled up within.

"Why?" David asked.

"If we venture out of here, there's a chance they might catch us. If we stay here, there's also a chance they still might catch us. Either way, I want to know that the evidence George died for is safely hidden." She screwed the lid back.

"Smart. No one would think to look inside an electrical junction box in a garage." He laughed. "Only an architect would think of—"

She sighed.

"Oh, right." David put his hand on her shoulder again. "Look, I'm sorry. I'm not buying that you believe architecture was your dad's dream for you, and I don't understand why your dad's death means you need to leave architecture—" he cleared his throat "—and me behind."

"I don't expect you to understand," she said, her voice steely.

He took the screwdriver from her hand, placed it back on the bench and turned her around to face him. "Then try me. Please."

"You won't understand. Knowing you, you'll make fun of me."

David sighed. "I don't deny I'm good at teasing

you—you give as good as you get too, you know—but I promise I won't make fun of your feelings."

Aria exhaled, her shoulders sagged. There was no avoiding it now. "Did you know that construction workers account for twenty percent of all on-the-job fatalities?"

David nodded.

"After seeing my dad fall like that, and knowing so many others face that same fate, I don't want to be a part of that world."

"But—"

She held up a hand. "We both know to be the kind of architect I'd want to be, I'd have to be on site a fair amount of time. And you… If I let us have a future that'd be opening myself up to the kind of pain I've watched my mom suffer and I…" Her eyes betrayed her as they filled with tears. "I can't do that," she whispered, shaking her head. "I'm just not strong enough."

David opened his mouth, frowned and pursed his lips. He pulled her into a hug and that weakened her reserve all the more. The floodgates opened. Tears for her dad, George and her mom all rushed to the surface.

"Can I ask you a question?" he asked.

She nodded against his chest.

"Did the site have a guardrail system, or was your dad using a personal fall arrest harness?"

Her words hit her like bricks. She shoved herself off his chest. "You think my dad's death was his own fault?" She bit out each word.

"No, no, I'm not saying that. Aria, it's just…yes, I know construction can be risky but what do you think I was learning in school? OSHA is there for a reason. There are tons of safety checks now, that if done…"

"I cannot believe I ever tried to talk to you."

"Listen. I only ask because sometimes these old-timers, my own dad included, make sure their employees are following all the new safety standards but since they're running the show, and they don't like to mess with all that falderal, they prefer to go it old-school."

She stared at the light within the lantern and ruminated over his words. "I don't know," she admitted. "But even if that is what happened, I don't see how that matters in the long run. Either way, I've made my decision."

"It matters because if we...if someday you wanted us to have another chance, then at least you could rest with the fact that I follow all the safety precautions. You'd have my word on that."

Aria couldn't believe she had just poured her heart out to a man who was using it to try to convince her...

David's eyes widened and he held out both hands. "Aria, I didn't mean... I wasn't trying to talk you into us." He groaned, took a step back and placed his hand on his forehead. "I'm no good at talking about feelings, Aria. Maybe that's why I like to take such stock in action meaning more than words. But let's not change the subject. Am I hearing you right that your goal now is to avoid all risk in life? Is that the bottom line?"

"No, no, no." She took a step toward him. "You did not just say that to me. I avoid risk? Aren't you the guy that *just* told me he waited years to share his feelings, only to put it in a card?"

His eyes narrowed. "Oh, I'm so sorry." But he didn't sound remotely apologetic. "I should've respected whatever convoluted reasoning you've cobbled together. Obviously, you've decided your feelings are more important than mine."

She gasped and even though he hadn't touched her, her cheeks heated so fast it was as if she'd been slapped. "Is that really what you think?"

"Does it matter what I think?" he shot back. His shoulders sagged. "No… I don't know. I'm sorry, Aria. I felt hurt and got defensive and said things I shouldn't have said."

She blinked the tears back and in an instant was able to put back up her emotional shield. "It's okay. We should've had that conversation two years ago, but I was too shut down, I guess. In some ways I still am. Maybe I always will be." She looked around the garage. "It's getting stuffy in here. I need some air." She strode out of the garage into the hallway. A buzzing noise reached her ears. Her phone!

FIFTEEN

"Aria?" David shouted after her. "What is it?" He grabbed the nail gun case and the battery charger and hustled after her. "We need to at least keep a weapon nearby."

She spun around, eyes wide, her phone in her hand. "It's my phone." She laughed. "Check yours!"

He powered up his cell.

"It's a bunch of texts," Aria said, her voice jubilant. "I've got five from my mom alone. She's used to me checking in three times a day. This could put her over the edge. I'm going to try calling the police again." She put her phone to her ear, but David could hear the error tones through the speaker before she could say anything.

"Network is still mostly busy," he said for her. "I imagine texts are easier to get through."

Her shoulders drooped. "It gives me hope, though. I'm going to try to respond to my mom." She bit her lip. "I don't think I can tell her what's going on. I'm not sure she could handle it without the doc increasing her meds first. These messages she's sending me… she's out of her mind with worry already, but maybe she can call the police for us?"

David's thumb froze on the screen. Her mother was on medication? She needed to check in three times a day? There must be a lot more going on in Aria's life than he had realized. "Hold off. If I can get a text to my dad or brothers, maybe they can reach the police for us without you increasing your mom's worry. Besides, my dad knows this area well." In answer, his phone also started vibrating with incoming messages from his friends and family and two texts from a number he didn't recognize. He'd read them as soon as he responded to his dad.

David tried to compress the message detailing their location and what had happened, but it still took four texts to get all the information conveyed. Within a minute he received a response:

Will do. We'll find a way to get to you. Stay safe. Dad.

He lifted his phone to allow Aria to see the screen. She put a hand to her chest. "I'm so thankful."

He turned back to his screen and read the first text from the unknown contact.

This is Valentina. George's wife. He left your number at house. Is he with you? Is he okay?

David fought a wave of nausea. He couldn't tell someone he'd never met that she was a widow over a text. That poor woman had to be worried sick, but he couldn't give her bad news this way. The next text jolted his heart.

Pls tell me if ur okay. Tried to find George. Two men with guns chased me. Can anyone help?

"Aria. Look at this. Do you think this is a group text?"

She peered over his shoulder and put a hand over her mouth. "I should've warned her."

He shook his head. "You tried, remember? The network was down and you didn't have her number. Focus on the next step. How should I respond?"

"Don't tell her about George yet. Ask her where she is and if she's somewhere safe."

His thumbs slid over the virtual keyboard. A moment later he was rewarded with a response.

Hiding alone. House north of state park. Scared. Only texts work. Can you help me? Please?!

Aria stood on her tiptoes, her chin grazing his shoulder as she read along. She took a step backward. "The good news is it sounds like she's safe for now, but we have to go to her, David. She's all by herself. She must be so scared. If she's just north of the state park, it's probably in walking distance. And there's more power in groups, right?"

He nodded. "Are we sure of her innocence?"

She twisted her lips to the side in a grimace. "No. Not a hundred percent." She took a deep breath. "But she's George's wife, and I know he loved her." Her breath hitched. "I really hate talking about him in the past tense."

David's stomach grew hot underneath his ribs. He

couldn't allow himself to grieve now, or he'd be of no use to Aria.

"While I'm not sure of her innocence," she continued, "I'm not sure of her guilt either. I couldn't live with myself if something happened to her when we could've—"

"If we help, we have to go with the mindset that it might be a trap."

Aria dropped her head. "I wish it was clear what to do."

David's phone buzzed. He read the text aloud.

Police can't get to you yet. Stay low until new plan. Mom calling in favors.

David paced in the hallway. "Sounds like the cavalry won't be coming anytime soon. So…we find out where this house is she's hiding in, but we be smart about it. First, we don't go to her until my nail gun is charged and…second, we need a way to test if it's a trap before entering."

"What do you mean?"

"Think about it. The possibilities include the men holding her hostage and making her send the messages, or her being in on it and trying to lure us to her. If we could rig some kind of distraction that would lead the gunmen out if they're with her, then we'd at least have a warning of what we were dealing with."

"I hadn't thought of that possibility," Aria admitted.

David grinned. "I think I have an idea, but I'll need your help."

Her eyes widened. "I know that mischievous look. What are you thinking?"

"It's a good thing I had a lot of brothers."

"David." Her voice had a hint of warning to it.

"Are you going to help me or not?"

She shrugged. "Just tell me what to do."

"Go back into the garage and bring me one of those emergency ice packs, but take care not to activate it yet."

She raised an eyebrow. "And then what are you going to do?"

"Add some more items to your list."

A smile emerged. "Such as?"

He took a deep breath. "Some non-salt seasoning, sugar…and I'll need to turn their fridge on for a little while."

She tilted her head and studied him. "We're on the clock."

"So get going," he said, not willing to reveal what he was up to.

She spun for the garage but after two steps gasped. "You're going to make a smoke bomb!"

He grinned. He knew she'd put together the pieces. It was one of the reasons he lov— David gulped and refocused. "Not one smoke bomb, Aria. That would make a pitiful distraction. We're going to make a whole set. Hurry. There's no guarantee our new buddies won't return."

Within a minute, she had joined him holding not one but two disposable freezer packs. He pointed to the supplies he'd gathered from the sparse pantry. At least the ingredients needed were considered staples in many homes. He looked up. "So you've done this before?"

She laughed. "Are you kidding? Dad hated to spend

money on anything he could make himself. Smoke bombs were a staple at our Fourth of July celebrations. I hated them—the smoke gives me a fierce headache—but the neighborhood kids seemed to enjoy them."

Aria slit the ice packs open with a knife and dissolved the ammonium nitrate in a glass bowl by stirring it up with the water from her bottle.

He set up a workstation on the counter next to the stove and prepared the rest of the ingredients. It hit him—Aria wasn't running away from risks. He had been dead wrong. Everything she did was the opposite—the flamethrower, a new career, even making these smoke bombs held some risk—but she was running from something. It was going to drive him crazy until he figured it out.

"Done," Aria proclaimed. "What's next?"

"Could you find some empty toilet paper rolls?"

She raised an eyebrow. "You're making them into smoke fountains?"

"The bigger the better," he said. "More chance to draw a crowd."

Aria rolled her eyes. "On it."

A half hour later their concoction resembled the texture and color of peanut butter—but definitely not the smell—and was setting up nicely in the freezer. "Now we wait."

Aria crossed the wooden floor to stand against the windows.

"It's so odd to see the stars—something so beautiful yet so normal—amid so much destruction and danger."

He checked on the battery charger for the nail gun. It was nearing full charge. He followed her to the wall of windows. "It's really not safe to hang out here. Too vulnerable."

"I won't stay long," she answered, her voice flat and dejected. Her fingertips brushed over the glass. "I wanted to see the stars and moon to remind myself that there's someone still in control, like you said. Everything feels so chaotic…so wrong."

He followed her gaze and marveled at the sight the moon afforded. The view revealed nothing but water and the tops of buildings. If he squinted he could make out large shapes drifting…wreckage of some sort. "My truck and tools are definitely gone forever," he said.

"I'm sure my car is too." She moaned. "I know you hated it, but I loved that thing. It served me well."

David almost reached out to her but managed the impulse and shoved his hands in his pockets instead. His thumb brushed against the sand dollar he had transferred from his wet clothes to the baggy jeans.

Years ago, Aria's mother—after the other parents had stopped lecturing them about the cave incident—had pulled Aria aside.

David had focused on the sand below his feet. As he bent down to dig up a half-buried sand dollar, he heard Aria's mom scold her for not getting out of the cave the moment she had discovered the tide.

"We thought about it, Mom, but David said we'd have risked getting our heads bounced around the rocks, trying to fight the current. He said we stood a better chance if we waited it out, and I agreed."

"I suppose I can understand that, but what on earth were you thinking trying out some unknown tunnel? You had no idea what you might have faced. We may have never found you." Her mother's voice shook.

David had acted as if he was still working in the sand but strained to hear every word as his gut burned with shame. Her mom wasn't too far off. It had been an impulsive and stupid situation. Only by the grace of God had they found a way out, but Aria's voice had held no hints of stress. "I was with David, Mom. He was leading the way."

Her mother unleashed a dramatic sigh. "He's just like your father, Aria, I hope you realize that—and he's a stubborn one to boot." The last few words were louder than the others, and David had been sure it was purposeful, for his benefit.

Aria had joined him. "I don't look anything like your father," David objected.

She released a lyrical laugh. "Oh, I know. She thinks saying that will deter me from you, but she made a big mistake. I happen to know my dad's got great qualities, and my mom's head over heels for him. Even after all these years."

"So he's stubborn?" David had asked.

She grinned. "Definitely." David had wanted to argue, as she had the same trait herself, but she continued. "But Dad's also resourceful, hardworking, witty, compassionate and…a genius in the field of construction. So, yeah, you two have some similarities."

David had smiled, satisfied with the answer. He finished brushing off the sand dollar. "For you, my lady." Her eyes had widened, and she had flashed a brilliant smile.

Now, as David held the shell in his hand, he wondered if she'd receive the sand dollar again with such joy. The resigned despair on her face as she stared out the window worried him. "There is one thing that's not lost to the waves," he said.

"Oh?" she asked, but her eyes didn't leave the scene past the windows.

"Aria, look at me," he said softly. He revealed the sand dollar in the palm of his hand.

She inhaled sharply. "How?" She reached out and caressed the top of the shell. He took her wrist with his other hand and flipped it so that the sand dollar transferred to her palm.

"The string was pretty flimsy," he answered. "But can you tell me why was it hanging in your car? Why'd you keep it?"

She inhaled. "Have you ever heard about the story behind the sand dollar?"

He tried not to laugh at her attempt to change the subject. "You're avoiding my question."

SIXTEEN

Aria's gaze never left the sand dollar. She had it preserved because it was the most romantic gift she'd ever received and it made her smile whenever she looked at it, but he didn't need to know that. "They say this flower shape here—" her finger drifted over the top of the shell "—looks most like an Easter lily. Then inside the center of the flower is the star of Bethlehem."

"That is extremely cool," David said, "but—"

"Oh, there's more," Aria continued, trying her best not to smile. He was so cute when his brow furrowed. She sobered at the next part. "The four holes represent the...the scars Jesus has in his hands and feet and side. But when you flip it—" she looked up to make sure she had David's attention and turned the sand dollar over "—the back looks like the Christmas flower."

He scrunched up his forehead. "The mistletoe?"

"No." She giggled. "The poinsettia. Look!" He stepped closer and bent down to see it in the little light that shone through the windows from the moon. "And...they say if you snap the sand dollar in half it'll break in a way that leaves you five doves so you can use them to spread goodwill and peace."

David pressed his lips together and nodded. "Pretty cool."

She sighed. "But for me, I love the sand dollar because it's so delicate yet it can withstand the waves hammering it from all sides...over and over. And the shell doesn't break until its occupant leaves it behind. It gives me hope that God made me to survive whatever life throws at me even though I feel like breaking."

Her eyelids fluttered to fight back the tears. She had meant to tell the story in order to keep things light and redirect the conversation but somehow her true emotions kept leaking out—literally, sometimes—in front of David. She inhaled deeply, then forced a laugh. "And then there are those who think they are mermaid coins."

Aria looked up, expecting to find David's laughing eyes, but instead his intense gaze locked on hers and he looked anything but amused. He lifted the string from her hand and looped it around her wrist so the sand dollar hung from it. Before she could ask him why, his hands slid over her jaw and behind her neck. He dipped his face and their lips touched.

His hand dropped to her back and pulled her closer. She rose on her toes to deepen the kiss, and the armor around her heart broke. To care and be cared for—oh, how she missed that. If only she could pretend they were just kids again. That there were no worries, no circumstances...

Three loud beeps reached her ears. Her heart dropped and she stumbled back. "What was that?"

His face paled. "I'm sorry. I couldn't stop thinking about mistletoe and how much I've missed you and—"

"No!" A laugh, deeper than anything she'd experienced in the past two years, erupted. "Not the kiss," she said, trying to stop laughing at his injured expression. "The...the beeping."

"Oh. That." He produced a sheepish grin that made him all the more attractive. Her heart was in serious trouble now.

"That was my phone." He slipped it from his pocket and groaned. She peeked to see the message from Valentina.

I think they've found me. Hiding in closet.

"Are the bombs ready?"

He shrugged. "I would've liked to give it more time for the potassium nitrate crystals to form, but I'll take what we can get. If she needs us, we go now. Help me wrap the underside in foil?"

Aria took long strides to the pantry and, after finding the foil, got right to work. "Text Valentina and ask her if she could describe her hiding place. If she can give us the house color or some kind of landmark it will help us find her faster. I don't know the north side as well as the south."

David nodded. A moment later the phone buzzed and they read the text together.

1521 Sunrise Blvd. Battery Almost Dead.

She watched David text an encouraging reply with a missive to stay put.

Aria ripped off a strip of tinfoil and wrapped it

around the underside of the smoke bomb. "Seems odd, don't you think?"

He joined her in the task. "What do you mean?"

"Do you know where we are? Do you know the address?"

He shrugged. "No, but I don't know the area as well."

"I've hiked these streets and trails for two years, and I don't know the addresses. I have a vague idea of the road names—I recognize Sunrise Boulevard—but even tonight, I didn't stop and look at the numbers by the door."

"If you were all alone and wanted someone to come and help, you might have paid more attention."

"Maybe," she acknowledged. "But it was also the speed in which she replied to you. Instantaneous. As if she had it copied and ready."

His fingers stilled. "You have a point. Are you changing your mind about going?"

She shook her head. "No. If there's a chance she's in danger, we need to help her. But your hostage theory seems more and more likely. I'm glad you thought of the smoke bombs."

His hands reached for hers. "Aria, I owe you an apology. It's clear to me you aren't running from risk."

She squeezed his hand and let go of him, but continued working, too shy to look up. "Thank you."

"And when I kissed you—"

"David," she warned. She really didn't want to start talking about their possible relationship right now.

"No, just let me finish. I know you don't want to start up where we left off so...so I will try to respect that, even though it's clear we're perfect for each other."

She let out an exasperated laugh. The man was stubborn.

"But I'm not trying to sway your opinion. Except it seemed like you wanted to kiss me just as much as I wanted—"

"David! Please!"

He held up his hands. "Just trying to communicate everything I'm thinking. Seemed you were really big on that earlier today."

"You know this isn't what I meant," she growled.

"But there's some truth to it," he said, his voice soft this time. "If I had just told you how much I loved you in person instead of in a card, then maybe you wouldn't have had to deal with your dad's passing alone. Maybe things would have been different."

Aria had suspected, maybe even hoped, that's what the card might have said. But by the way he carried on today she hadn't wanted to believe it. Her vision blurred, which didn't take much in the low light conditions.

"Did you…did you ever love me too?" he asked.

"Of course I did." She jerked her focus to the windows. She hadn't meant to raise her voice. "But…but things have changed, circumstances have changed. Sometimes you don't get to have everything you want because it might not be the best decision in the long run."

"What I want or what you want?"

Aria balled her hands up in fists. It seemed as if he was trying to trick her into saying something, but she didn't have anything to hide. She had told him every-thing. "Does it matter, David?"

"It depends," he answered. "Are you staying away from me and architecture for your sake or your mom's sake?"

Aria's mouth fell open. She had never considered… but she was so tired and her emotions so confused she honestly didn't know. There was a time that she admired and loved how David always went for what he wanted. He wasn't passive, given to waiting for things to work themselves out. He was a man of ac-tion. Usually, she preferred that, but tonight she was so weary she wanted him to give up without a fight. Besides, even if she was able to analyze and explain in detail all her reasoning, he still might not agree with it. This was partly—or maybe mostly—her fault. She should've never kissed him back. Her lips burned at the memory. She shook her head. "I can't separate it right now, and I'm afraid you're just going to have to accept that."

David stared at her for a moment before he nodded.

Aria breathed a sigh of relief. He had let it go for now.

"Daylight will be here before we know it. That was the last smoke bomb. Are you ready?"

"No," Aria answered truthfully. "But I'll go any-way." She grabbed her bag but after fingering the heavy laptop, she realized it would only weigh her down. David filled his tool belt with the prepared smoke fountains and a lighter. He lifted the nail gun, made sure it was fully stocked, hooked it on a loop on his right side and led the way out the front door.

"Wait." She fingered the note she had revised on the counter. "Do you have any cash?"

He laughed and pulled out several twenty-dollar bills. "Wow. You have a lot of cash." She placed them on the counter, underneath her note, and followed him. "I'll pay you back my portion as soon as I can get to a bank."

"Aria kidding me?" he asked, chuckling at himself. "Seriously, don't worry about it. I always stock up on cash before I travel. When we get back home, we'll contact the owners and make sure everything gets squared away." He opened the door but held a hand out, indicating she should wait and let him go first. After a moment he nodded and opened the door wider. "I think it's clear," he whispered.

She set her laptop against the side of the house underneath the porch overhang. If they got out of this alive, maybe she could pick it up later. It was doubtful the hard drive was still intact, but she'd like to at least make an effort to see if anything could be salvaged.

"Do you know which way to go? There's not enough network available to let us use the map features on our phones. I checked." David grabbed her hand and squeezed.

"I think so. The state park is nine miles wide near the highway. It's more narrow here, which means we'll need to go off the beaten path to get there faster."

"So be prepared to crawl over fallen trees?"

"Maybe. I think there's a thin trail to the west that should take us where we want to go. If I'm remembering right, that is."

"I think we better go back to the no-light policy, but I brought the flashlight with me just in case."

She took a big breath and let her eyes acclimate to the outdoors. Mentally, she tried to get her bearings and picture where Sunrise Boulevard was from their location. Once she was sure they weren't being watched, she tugged on his warm hand and they entered the dark forest once again.

SEVENTEEN

David figured they had walked forty-five minutes in silence. The quiet was making him sleepy, and the fog that had settled on the ground made it even harder to see each step in front of them. At least she was still willing to hold his hand. He'd already kept her upright three times and she'd helped him not fall on his face… well, who was keeping score anyway?

If Aria felt anything like he did, then she was too exhausted to keep up conversation anyway. "I'm starting to wonder if we should've stayed the night and rested before trying to find her."

"Me too," Aria admitted with a sigh. "But if I'm leading us where I think, then we've got a fifteen-minute walk ahead of us. That's it. And I figure we have a better shot at helping her escape in the dark than the light."

"Agreed. It's too late to turn back around anyway."

"So what exactly is the plan? I'd feel a lot better if we knew how this was going down."

He shrugged. "What's to plan? If we see the Hummer, we know we're dealing with a hostage situation. We light the smoke bombs underneath their car. When they run out, I shoot them with the nail gun…probably aiming at their legs so they can't continue to chase us. We rescue Mrs. Swanson, run away and hide somewhere else until the cops can help."

Aria put her palms against the sides of her face. "First off, I know she's Mrs. Swanson, but could we just refer to her as Valentina? I know it's not fair to her, but whenever I hear the name Mrs. Swanson, I think of Barbara."

"Yeah, I get that—she made the best cookies in the lobby. Better than my grandma's cookies, but don't tell anyone that. Remember the oatmeal butterscotch ones?"

Aria put a hand on her stomach and a loud gurgle erupted in the forest. "More than ever. I'm hungry again. New rule—no talking about food. Second, could we come up with a less gruesome plan? Shooting those guys in the legs sounds so medieval."

David crossed his arms over his chest. "What did you have in mind? You want me to shoot their pant leg, taking care not to hit any flesh, but still trapping them to a post?"

"I'm guessing by your tone that's not a very likely scenario?"

David laughed. "Aria, I haven't even taken this thing for a practice round. And I'm not a teenager anymore. I don't spend time shooting rounds in my dad's garage for fun. There are no more contests with my brothers."

The hard-packed dirt trail widened and a layer of mulch covered the remainder of the path. "We must be getting close," Aria commented. "So let's stop now."

She pointed at a sign ten feet in front of them. "I think it's time to work in a little practice."

David raised an eyebrow. "You're serious?"

"Aim for the first letter." She squinted. "I can't really tell what it says from here."

"In this fog and lighting, I can barely see it at all." He lifted the nail gun off the tool belt. "I have it set up for fast succession. Did you know this puppy can shoot sixty nails per minute? The magazine holds six hundred. Of course I can probably only get that much out of the battery charge, but it would be a pretty intense ten minutes."

"Will the gunmen know there's that kind of time limit on it?"

He pursed his lips. "Let's hope not. Give me a minute. I'm switching the drive to a single shot instead of rapid succession. I need to disable the safety. Normally you have to press down into the surface to get it to shoot."

"I'm aware," she said.

David tilted his head right to left to loosen up his neck muscles. Of course she knew that. He flicked the switch, removed the safety and exhaled.

Ka-ching. Dirt flew up ten feet away.

Aria gasped.

"Pretty safe to say I'm a bit rusty."

"Looks like it."

"Would you like to take a shot, my lady?" he retorted.

"I was merely agreeing with you. Please continue."

David stared at her a moment and recalled her teasing about being the fastest nail gun shooter in the West. Even years ago she had a sly smile about her when he relayed his ability and stories about shooting practice. Why hadn't he seen it before? "You're a good shot, aren't you?"

"What do you mean?"

There it was. More of her evasive techniques. He grinned. "I should've known, growing up with your dad…"

Her lips twisted to the side, confirming his suspicions. "I knew it."

"David, it was a long time ago," she said.

"No, no. The least you could do is show me now."

"I told you I don't want anything to do with…"

"Yeah, I've heard you and I don't buy it. The least you could do is save my pride by showing me what you got."

She huffed then stepped to the side. "Fine. But Dad didn't teach me to shoot one of these."

"What did you shoot then?"

"My dad loved going to the shooting range. He had an assortment of guns." She flashed an apologetic smile. "Real guns."

"I see. Well, I'm man enough not to be threatened by a woman that can shoot better than me. Have at it."

She took a step away from him. "You've been warned."

Ka-ching. The branches to the left fifteen feet ahead shook, startling her. She took a step back and then *pow, pow, pow.*

"Whoa. Hold on. Hold on." He held his hands out. "Hopefully all the trees give us some sound barrier, but it's still not quiet."

She handed the gun back to him. "It's not as loud

as I thought it would be either. Certainly not as loud as a 45-caliber. You have the safety back on?"

He nodded.

"Then I want to see how I did." She hustled to the sign and held her phone up to the wood.

David quickened his step and let out a small groan. She had hit the first three letters of the sign. Right in the middle. "I want a rematch," he said. "You got a warm-up shot. I think I should too."

They ran back and this time he made his mark each time.

"Feel better?"

"As a matter of fact, I do. And if we're going to face guys with real guns, a little confidence can go a long way."

"Good. Because even if I was a better shot, there's no way I would be able to shoot at those gunmen. That gun is too heavy for me to go more than a few shots."

He slipped the safety on and reattached the gun to the belt. "Fair enough. Speaking of which, we should keep moving. If they did hear us, no doubt they'll want to investigate."

"We're still a good mile away. No way anyone heard us." She trekked forward at a much faster clip than they had previously set. The adrenaline from shooting practice seemed to have taken the place of caffeine. They both were more awake and alert.

Aria groaned. He caught up to her and found her with her phone in her face. "What is it?"

"I missed a text from my mom again. She's losing it. I'm sure she's not getting any sleep. She walks a tight enough line as it is. I keep trying to text her back, and it keeps failing."

"Network down again?"

"Or my phone has too little a charge to hold the signal." She held it up and he saw the small sliver of red left. Then it went black. Her shoulders sagged. "Great. Now I have no phone."

"Do you want me to try?"

"No."

He frowned. If it was that important then why didn't she want his help? "Would it upset your mom more if it came from me?"

"Probably."

For reasons he couldn't explain, his heart rate increased. He added up everything she had told him about the past two years. "So, you had to break the news to your mom, she wouldn't go home…did you have to call the movers too? Arrange for the house to sell?"

She waved a hand at him. "I don't think we have time for this right now."

"You check in with her three times a day… Aria, did you abandon architecture so it wouldn't remind your mom of your dad? Did you leave everything behind that could possibly remind her of him to keep her from pain?"

"I don't expect you to understand," Aria said.

"I think I'm beginning to understand. You never grieved," he proclaimed. "You were never given a chance."

She spun around so fast on the spot his hands rose up in a defensive position. "You have no idea how much I've grieved."

"That's just it," he answered. "How can you possibly work through it if you're avoiding everything that reminds you of him? I was so wrong. You're not running from risk, you're running from grief, but instead of offering escape, it's trapping you there." David could relate a little, only because he remembered how he felt after their relationship ended. "Do you know why I went to that two-year construction management program? It wasn't because I needed it. After we broke up I couldn't stand to interact with any architect. And you know why? Because they reminded me of you. Dad said he couldn't let me take over his business when I was too busy losing it for him. He was going to have to fire me, until Mom talked me into going back to school. To give me some time away, some time to heal."

"This—" she pointed her finger "—this is why I couldn't talk to you." She shook her head. "I knew... I just knew you wouldn't let it go."

She twisted away and stomped off. David clenched his fists. There he went again—his pride had to find a reason that made sense to him why she didn't want to be with him and he kept pushing. His mom always said he could use his stubborn persistence for good or bad. Seemed to be erring on the wrong side lately.

He ran to catch up with her. "Aria, please—" he put a hand on her shoulder "—I'm sorry. You're right. I overstepped and wasn't respecting your wishes. I can't seem to accept what-ifs and fear as a reason we can't be together."

"But when I didn't respond to your card in the right way, that seemed to be enough for you—"

"Because I thought you didn't love me! But now... I mean, if there was someone else I could understand—"

"Let it go, David."

His heart twinged. Yet something seemed off. "I will, but just tell me this. Why'd you kiss me?"

Aria released an exasperated sigh. "I did not kiss you. It was all you and your misguided mistletoe thoughts. And we're getting closer. Could you lower your voice?"

David crossed his arms over his chest and remembered her gentle kiss. He knew he hadn't imagined her reaction to him, but in the end, did it matter? She didn't want to be with him. He had to accept it, even if it required that she beat him over the head until it sank in. He nodded. "No problem."

Ten minutes later, they stepped out of the forest clearing, away from mulch and onto asphalt. He heard the surf crashing against the rocks down below. "At the first sign of a car or a house, it's off the trail and back into the forest. Agreed?"

"Agreed."

The curve revealed the first house. He peeked around an especially tall fern and sighed. From the seven or eight looming shadows he assumed were houses, only one had a light glowing from within—presumably a lantern or flashlight. "She's either not the brightest bulb—excuse the pun—or this is most definitely a trap."

"We don't know for sure it's the address yet," Aria said, her voice light. "Maybe it's a local who actually stuck around, although I'd be surprised." They crept closer, and he squinted until he could see the numbers. "It's the house," she groaned.

The brown shapes to the right caught his attention. "Look. The rest of the line seems to be in the middle of construction."

"Luxury condo rentals for tourists," she interrupted. "Judging by the design of the framing." She shook her head. "Not that it matters."

As much as this woman claimed to be done with architecture, the little bit of longing in her voice said otherwise. It was a shame she couldn't see it. So far, they hadn't spotted any cars.

Since the garage had no windows, he couldn't peek in there to look for the Hummer. He studied the small Victorian house—it looked half the size of the house they'd chosen to hide in. Two stories for sure, but the way the roof slanted meant the top floor only had one or two bedrooms at most. If he had to hide there, where would he pick? There wouldn't be many options unless it was filled with furniture of the time period, or they abandoned the theme and put in walk-in closets.

He supposed they should alert Valentina so she would know they were there, but only if they took care of the gunmen first. The bad guys could have her phone.

"Stay here," he told Aria. "I'll set the smoke bombs. If the gunmen are here, wait until I'm able to disarm them, then go in after Valentina." He held up a hand as she inhaled, knowing she was about to argue. "I promise I will try not to shoot their actual legs but, Aria, I'm going to do what I have to do."

"That's great, but I'm not waiting here for you to go be an action hero and get yourself killed. We'll have a better shot if we do this together. When it's two guns versus rapid-fire nails, timing will be everything." She pointed to the center of her chest. "I'll light the smoke bombs while you hide and wait to catch them off guard. If you get behind them maybe you could talk them into dropping their weapons before any violence. And if that doesn't work, what if you released thirty seconds of rapid succession nails as a warning shot? Right down the middle?" She blinked up sweetly at him. "I'm sure at that range you can't miss."

He tilted back his head and laughed silently. Her feistiness always caught him off guard. "Good one. Fine. We'll do it your way, but with a little bit of variance. Since the smoke bombs don't make any sound, set them up below the front bay windows. I'll shoot out the window, then run to the porch and wait for them to exit. You go around the back and sneak into the house and find Valentina." He pulled the cables from his tool belt. "I'll restrain our new buddies with these."

"Zip ties? Where'd you get those?"

"The garage, when I was loading up extra nails. I thought they might be useful."

Aria bit her lip. "It's a great plan, unless Valentina is the one who runs out the front…all by herself, and in that case, we've just shot out a beautiful window for no reason."

David lowered his voice. "No, it'll be for a reason. It's my best idea at keeping you safe. I don't want to see a man shoot at you ever again, Aria. I've never been so scared in my life as when I had to drag you out of that lobby. If it turns out Valentina is all alone, then all the better. I'll gladly accept the consequence for the broken window."

Her face sobered and she stared right into his eyes. "Okay," she whispered. "We do it your way." He turned to walk away when she grabbed his wrist. "And for the record, this is the kind of communication I was referring to earlier. Thank you."

EIGHTEEN

Aria fought to focus on the task at hand. Her mind was still warring between rage and shock at David's analysis in the forest. Did his words hold any truth? Was she running from grief?

"What are we waiting for?" David asked.

The wind brushed against her face. "Nothing." She darted out of the woods and toward the window. A white sweater was the worst possible thing to wear when trying to blend into the night. She felt David's presence beside her until she knelt down onto the rocky landscape in front of the bay window.

She looked up, and he was gone. Hiding. Suddenly every cracking twig and swaying branch in the area screamed danger. The wind teased her hair up as she fumbled with setting the bombs in such a way that they wouldn't tip over the moment she let go.

Aria shifted so her back would shield most of the wind.

"Hurry," David whispered urgently. She couldn't see him but knew he had picked a spot where he could keep an eye on her.

The plan was to avoid a lungful of smoke, but she

needed to stay close until she was sure the flame had taken effect. *Please be with us in this, Lord.* She cupped her hand and lit the smoke bomb fountains, one by one.

While the wind didn't halt, it did lessen. She crinkled her nose. If breaking the window wouldn't get anyone's attention, the smell of the smoke bombs certainly would. It smelled like a dozen rotten eggs went to a party with a scared skunk as an escort.

The foil wrapped around the bottom would force the smoke to shoot higher and higher, and she wasn't waiting around for that. She darted down the side and around the house, inhaling copious amounts of fresh, salty air.

Crash.

David had shot out the window. So far, everything was going to plan. *Please let this all be for nothing. Let Valentina be inside and the gunmen far, far away...*

She halted at the corner. Now that she was away from the trees, the moon illuminated the sharp dropoff on this side of the outcropping. It wasn't a cliff but more like a steep hill covered in mammoth black boulders that usually led down to the beach. Instead she could make out the ocean more than halfway up the hill. Aria was almost sure there used to be more rock and land directly behind these structures. Room enough to set deck chairs and enjoy the view.

She inhaled sharply. Which meant there had been landslides. It wasn't too shocking given the earthquake and tsunami. She just hoped she was standing on solid ground. Her hands pressed up against the siding, even though there was nothing she could grip. She sidestepped her way to the back deck steps.

A series of thuds reached her ears. "You take the front, I'll go out the back."

Her feet slipped on the landscaping rock. She regained her equilibrium in time to flatten herself against the side of the porch steps. Her heart pounded so hard it made her rib cage ache. No, no, no. There was no contingency plan for this. No one was supposed to go out the back. The smoke and noise was from the front. *Follow the noise*, she wanted to yell.

But she was out in the open, wearing a white sweater, without any weapon. She wasn't sure what to do. The story of David and Goliath came to mind, but she didn't think that was pertinent, except…rocks. She didn't have a sling, but she had an arm, and hopefully adrenaline would help her throw better than she pitched. She never thought she'd live to see the day that she'd regret not going out for the community softball league. There was no time to sort rocks and pick the best ones. Aria bent over and grabbed two of the biggest ones she spotted and straightened.

The man ran down the steps, shaking the foundation she had pressed up against. His back was to her as he ran toward the very corner she'd just come from, gun out and up. The temptation to let him run past her was strong. After all, he didn't seem to have seen her, but he was also running right to David.

It was now or never. She pictured David surrounded by gunmen and that was all the motivation she needed. She would not let another loved one be killed when she had the power to stop it.

She inhaled as she pulled the rock behind her neck, then exhaled as her hips twisted with power. She put every bit of strength into the baseball-sized rock's projection. The moment it left her fingertips she held her breath. The rock sailed in an arc and slammed directly between the man's shoulders.

He didn't fall or drop unconscious—as she had hoped—but he bent over, hollering so loud she prayed David could hear him. It was as close a warning as she could give. She didn't wait for the man to look for his attacker. She sprinted up the steps with one rock remaining in her hand in case she needed it.

She flung open the back door, trying to shut it behind her quietly. She didn't think the gunman had seen her or he'd have likely shot at her. Aria flipped the dead bolt for good measure until she remembered they'd already broken the front window. Yeah, so locks were useless. "Valentina?" she tried to yell in a whisper. There was no sense alerting the men back inside. If they had any chance of rescuing her and getting out aloud, she needed to play it fast...and smart.

Aria tiptoed at a runner's pace through each room, searching for any sign of George's wife. She saw through the broken window where David was hiding, waiting, except he wasn't seeing the gunman taking aim at him from the opposite corner. Without thinking she threw the second rock straight through the broken hole in the window, directly at the gunman's head. Her heart sank when she thought she'd missed until she saw the man's shoulder jerk back with a howl. David spun and aimed the nail gun at him. "Lay down your weapon."

Unfortunately the gunman had his gun still pointed at David and just growled back at him. "Not on your life." They were at a standstill and looking so hard at each other they weren't paying attention to her, which meant she needed to hurry and find Valentina and go help him before the other gunman joined him.

She eyed the wooden stairs and approached with trepidation. The second level wouldn't have any exits. But Valentina wasn't on the first floor so there wasn't much choice. She took a deep breath and sprinted up the steps. She wished she had one more rock left, but instead she was defenseless.

The first bedroom and the bathroom were empty but the second bedroom was located in the back. It had two large windows facing the ocean-side view. The moonlight's beam pointed directly at the full-size bed. On it lay a woman's body—still and unmoving— with black hair spilling over the pillow. Aria flung a hand to her mouth. In jeans and a dark sweater she recognized as one of George's favorites, this had to be Valentina. Aria rushed to the bed. Her fragile form made Aria wonder if she was too late. Had they already killed her?

"Valentina?" When she put a hand on her wrist to search for a pulse, the woman's blank face turned toward her. Aria exhaled. "You're alive." Valentina's eyes didn't betray any emotion. It was the look of devastation, of loss. She knew that look all too well. Her mother had been wearing it daily for the past two years. Valentina was a broken woman, a wife in mourning. All doubts that Valentina could've been behind George's murder faded.

"You know about George," Aria whispered. It wasn't a question. His murderers were sure to have bragged about it. Aria's blood pumped hotter and faster, furious.

Valentina blinked and turned her face back to the

window, staring at the moon. Aria grabbed her arm. "George wouldn't want you to give up and die. You have to fight. You have to get out of here. Come with me!" Valentina cooperated, although wordlessly.

Valentina stood up and shook off Aria's grip. "He always said he wanted his last breath to be at that place." Her voice was cold and monotone.

Aria jerked to a stop, the memory of George being shot hitting her full-force. She blinked rapidly, her eyes stinging. She could mourn later. She'd said that to herself so often she wondered for a split second if David was right. Was she stuck in a trap between holding on to grief and not being able to fully experience it? David…"We have to get you out of here now. David is in danger. I need to help him."

She nodded and followed Aria down the stairway, albeit at a slower rate than ideal. The woman was probably still in shock. "Did the men tell you why they were keeping you here?" Aria whispered.

Valentina didn't answer. Aria reached the landing and started looking around the foyer for a weapon to help David out. "Well, don't worry. Because once we get out of here, I have enough evidence to put these guys behind bars forever."

Aria unplugged the lamp at the entry table. It would do in a pinch. She peeked out the broken window but didn't see David and the gunman, though it was possible they'd moved to the other side of the porch.

Valentina hadn't followed her, though. The woman was paralyzed, one hand on the banister, but her stone face had morphed into surprise. "What do you mean?"

"Huh? Oh, just trust me."

"Are you sure? What kind of evidence?"

Aria wished she hadn't opened her mouth at all. A wife in mourning can only think about her husband, not other more practical matters, apparently— like avoiding getting killed. She tugged on the sleeve of Valentina's sweater. "I'll explain if you keep moving." Valentina complied and stayed at her side as they snuck back to the rear exit. "George kept records and did his own sleuthing when he started to suspect something. I haven't gone through it all yet, I just know he has enough to take down whatever scam these guys were running."

She put one hand on the door handle and looked straight into Valentina's eyes. "Do you have a weapon? Because otherwise you're going to have to focus on running…no more slow walking." She studied Valentina's face. A ripple of emotions had caused her to breathe heavy. "Maybe we should try the garage," Aria muttered.

"So the evidence didn't wash away with the tsunami?"

"No," Aria said, waving her hand. "But we can discuss all that later. Let's go."

"I can't let you do that."

Aria looked down and found Valentina pointing a gun straight at her heart.

NINETEEN

They were at a standoff, and David wasn't sure what the next move would be. If it hadn't been for Aria making him promise not to shoot the man in the back, this wouldn't have been an issue, but the gunman who had been punched in the nose, had his suit set on fire and been fumed to pass out, was a little mad. Just a little. And a whole lot determined.

"There's no way I'm putting down my weapon," the man said, his voice shaking with rage. "And I'm not killing you straight away either. This won't be easy for you."

Nothing about this week was going right for David—why should he have assumed his plan would? He wasn't scared by the man's threats, though. He'd seen guys mad—he had three brothers after all—and he could tell when a guy was talking smack or not. This man was exaggerating about killing him slowly. Not that he wasn't going to kill him, though. No, that was certain. Unless David shot him first. Which meant there was only one thing to do…stall him until he had a plan.

David kept the nail gun level at his chest just as the

gunman kept his 22-caliber pointed at David's head. David's back was pressed against the far eastern pillar holding up the porch so that he could see if anyone was coming from his backside. David let his eyes dart around his surroundings, praying for a solution. *And please help Aria rescue George's wife, Lord.*

He wasn't one of those guys who worked better under pressure. David needed to relax, pretend this was a bully and let his mind run with it. David sighed. "Well, if you're going to have fun with it, seems like we should at least have introductions. I'm David McGuire, and you are?"

The gunman frowned a half second, taken aback by the question. It was the pause that David needed. On the rapid contact setting, he pressed the trigger. The nail gun did not disappoint. It hit the man's gun barrel with enough force to wrench it out of his hands and back. Unfortunately, on the rapid setting the nails kept firing even as he let up on the trigger. The nails attacked up and over the man's head and then, as David was trying to stop it, in a straight line down and into the porch. Another gunman—the guy Aria referred to as Robert—rounded the corner, gun out. Robert hollered and a shot rang out, painfully close to David's right ear. The pain was excruciating, and the stinging in his head wouldn't stop.

On instinct, David turned and sprinted into the darkness, past the large tree separating the house from the condo construction. He couldn't trust himself to aim and shoot with any accuracy due to the pain. He kneeled down behind the trunk, dropped the nail gun and pressed against his right ear with all the pressure he could give. If only he could ease the throbbing.

His hand was wet. He tentatively felt with his finger and his head started to spin at the realization a notch out of the top of his ear was missing. Below it the ear was already starting to swell. He prayed the cartilage hadn't shattered.

He could still hear with his left ear, although it was hard to focus when his other eardrum seemed to be throbbing with the rush of blood to the area.

"Go after him!" the gunman yelled at Robert. "Where's my gun?"

"I think it went by the window. He's in the trees. I'm not going after him without a flashlight. I think I got a shot on him, so he should be easier to track."

"She says she has evidence," a female voice interjected.

David dared to peek around the trunk. They had Aria. The plan, getting shot, it was all for nothing. He gritted his teeth. Pain or not, he needed to get to a better vantage point if he had any hope of rescuing her.

He squinted at the building behind him. While without drywall, the framing seemed to be finished and there was a giant opening just above the leaves of the tree he was hiding behind. If he could get up there, he might get a better shot at the men…and the woman with the gun. He shook his head. If that woman was George's wife—the betrayal he felt for his departed friend produced another surge of adrenaline. He clenched his jaw, jumped to his feet, and while keeping his back low in case they could see him through the hanging foliage, darted to the back of the condo building.

He walked through the open door and the smell of wood soothed him. He was at home on a construction site, and it gave his level of courage a boost. Taking the steps in front of him by two he reached the third level in seconds. If he went to the front of the building he would be just over the treetop enough that he should be able to get a decent shot, as long as he was fast and they hadn't moved yet.

They wouldn't stand out in the open for long, although the Robert guy did seem to be under the impression David was the type of man to run. That may have been true in his younger years, but that was one thing that had changed. Now, he was the type of guy who would stand his ground and fight for what mattered.

If he bent a knee at the edge of the framing he'd be right above the treetop with a clear shot and... David shook his head. Mere hours ago he had promised Aria that he always followed safety protocol. But this was different. He was trying to save Aria and there was no time to waste. He argued with himself for half a second until he spotted something shining off the reflection of the full moon. A personal fall arrest system hung from the middle of the building, between what would be two different apartments. It was a top-of-the-line system, which meant it would be very easy to use. He sighed and made fast work of slipping on the attached harness.

The system hung from a steel rod installed straight into the ground and would, theoretically, be able to hold five thousand pounds. A man of his size, if he fell from six feet up, would create a force close to two thousand pounds, which was why so many severe injuries happened with falls of that nature. He guessed he was standing over twenty feet above the ground.

If set up correctly, and he fell, the system wouldn't let him drop more than six feet.

The harness snug on his body, he bent down low and snuck to the edge of the frame. The pulley system resembled a retractable leash as it let out enough line for him to continue to walk. David took a deep breath, wobbling a bit. His sense of balance was a little off as his ear continued to throb in rhythm to his heart rate.

"She's right. I have evidence." He heard Aria's voice drift up. She spoke to the men sternly, her volume rising. "And I'm not the only one who knows where I've hidden it."

"You referring to the guy I just shot? Cause I guarantee he's not going far before I finish him off."

David dropped to one knee. He could barely see over the branches. He had intended to lie on his stomach for more support, but it seemed that wasn't an option.

"No, he's not the only one," she challenged. "Besides, he doesn't know anything. He's just a new hire that happened to get in the way."

David smiled. She was trying to protect him, stall and keep them talking. He shifted the nail gun drive to single-shot mode, afraid an errant rapid fire round might end up striking Aria. He balanced his elbow on his left knee and tried to take aim. The question was, where would he shoot first?

"Is that so?" Robert replied. "Then why was he helping you?"

"Because he has good manners," she snapped.

Robert took a step forward and straightened into a threatening posture. David tried to steady his shot, but he was too close to Aria for comfort.

"I can vouch for that," the strange woman answered. "He was a new hire. George had said he wouldn't arrive until late today."

"Bad timing on his part because it doesn't matter," Robert growled. "He's still a liability."

"Who else knows where the evidence is hidden?" the woman interjected.

Aria raised her chin. "I sent a text to a policeman friend."

"That's easy enough to check." Robert pulled the bag away from Aria and took a step closer to the porch light as he shuffled inside for her phone.

It was the chance he needed. David aimed for the gun in Robert's hand. He shot...and missed. The nail hit Robert's forearm. He released a guttural scream. The other man jumped back on the porch, having apparently found his gun.

The thug ignored Robert's scream and pointed his gun in David's direction. David was sure they couldn't see him, but it apparently didn't matter to the gunman. The guy gritted his teeth, raised his arm diagonally and started shooting blindly—on a death mission.

David spun around to change location. A bullet pierced his right shoulder. He screamed as his flesh ripped apart. The pain sent him reeling sideways. His foot twisted and he found himself falling backward. His arms flailed, trying to regain equilibrium. The nail gun slipped from his fingers. But it was too late, he was falling, and with a sickening crunch his backside hit something hard. Whatever he had hit was breaking away underneath his weight. It gave way, and he was airborne again.

TWENTY

Aria tried to lunge for the gunman's arm, but Valentina shoved the gun barrel deeper into her lower back, at the same time as she dug her fingernails into Aria's upper arm. Aria arched her back in pain but stopped trying to move. A crash grabbed her attention. In the dim light she saw the shadow of a man fall from above the tree. The nail gun hit the ground followed by a six-foot figure. "No," she cried. "David!"

Her lungs stopped working. She couldn't breathe. Her chest went into spasms. Her eyes stung. *Not again, not again*. She lurched forward to go to him but Valentina's steel grip held her back. "It will do no good."

"Kirill, help me!" Robert barked. He gripped his hand, moaning, a nail sticking from his forearm. Kirill rushed to Robert's side and helped him up. He ushered his boss inside but looked over his shoulder before the door closed. "Get the girl inside. Then use a flashlight and see if he's really dead."

The last word sent a shiver down Aria's spine. Tears that fell without reservation grew to sobs. Aria couldn't hold herself up any longer, and Valentina didn't try to stop her as she sunk to her knees, her head in her hands.

"So that was a lie," Valentina said. "You knew him."

The pain was crushing Aria's rib cage. She wanted to die. At least her dad knew she had loved him with all her heart. At least George knew of her loyalty and devotion. But David…she'd told herself she couldn't be with him to avoid what seemed like the inevitable, and instead…her worst fears had come true anyway. And right in front of her eyes. She wished she could have taken back the two years without him. Tears spilled onto her sweater. "I loved him," she croaked. Aria looked up through hazy vision at Valentina. "Like I thought you loved George," she sneered.

Valentina's features hardened. "Don't. You have no idea how much I loved that man. But he…he loved that place too much. He could've taken the money they were going to give us and we would've been happy, but he chose. He chose that place over me."

Aria shook his head. "But they're not out to kill you. You're part of this. You arranged the whole thing," Aria said, putting the pieces together. "I knew George would've never agreed to sign a contract like that without someone he trusted encouraging him to do it. He did it for you," she accused. "If you loved him, you would've known he was a man of integrity. He'd never have turned a blind eye to this."

The mask of pain she'd seen Valentina bear earlier returned. "Get inside. We aren't done with you."

"Why should I do anything you want? You killed him."

"I didn't kill him," she screeched. Valentina's arm shook as she raised the gun to Aria.

Aria shook her head. "You played your part. And they'll kill me too, as soon as I give them what they want." Aria stood on shaking legs, anger fueling her muscles. "They're going to kill you too, Valentina. Make amends," she challenged. "If you loved him at all, like you say, bring justice to George's death." Her voice broke and the tears blurred her vision again. The only thing that kept her fighting at that moment was the thought of her mother at home, sick with worry. She needed to live, for her.

"They won't kill me," Valentina replied, her voice thick. "And if you help, I promise they won't kill you." Her eyes darted to the side and Aria knew she was lying.

"You can't promise such a thing, can you?"

"Hush," Valentina ordered. She pulled out a phone and turned on the flashlight setting. "Save yourself more pain and look away."

Aria couldn't tear her eyes away, though. The beam of light swept past the tree trunk to the nail gun on the ground, and to a figure covered by branches and…and David's shirt. Valentina shut off the light. "I'm sorry," she said. "There's nothing you can do for him now."

"I saw Kirill kill George too," Aria said. Her only weapon was her words. "Shot your husband point-blank."

Valentina's gaze snapped back to Aria's, her eyes widening.

"He loved you, you know," Aria said, knowing it was true but would also serve as a more painful blow than any fist could. "He told me himself."

Tears welled up in Valentina's eyes. "Get inside," she hissed. She leaned down and swiped up Aria's bag. Robert had dropped it the moment the nail hit his forearm. Valentina straightened and shoved Aria through the open front door with the pistol in her back. Aria cried out at the same time Valentina slammed the door behind them.

David had never been so thankful for adrenaline. He had heard stories about people being able to do amazing things while it pumped through their veins, but now he understood. It was the only thing keeping him moving, the only thing keeping him from passing out from the pain in his shoulder and his ear. He had to save Aria before it was too late.

He peeked around the wide trunk only to watch Aria and Valentina reenter the house.

The moment he had stepped on that top floor, eager to save her, he had regretted his promise to Aria. But if he hadn't stayed true to his word and put on the safety gear, he'd be a dead man by now. And if it hadn't been for this blessed tree, he'd have been shot to death. He'd give God the praise for that one.

When he had fallen, it had broken a thick branch... about six feet in length. He had reached out and found another branch and hung on as the log crashed to the ground.

Aria's haunting cry still gave him chills. He had no doubt that she had assumed the shadowed figure on the ground was him, not a broken part of the tree. He had wanted to call out, to assure her he was okay— well, maybe not okay, but alive at least—but with his weapon on the ground, that would've been foolish. David had been hanging in the air, amid the remaining tree branches, when he heard the Kirill guy order

Valentina to use a flashlight to check that he was dead. Aria proceeded to start an argument with her.

It was an odd sensation, kind of like witnessing his own funeral, except Aria was showing no sign of restraint. Although she didn't realize he was still alive, her passionate zeal was helping the situation. It gave him time to prepare. *Keep her talking, sweetheart.*

Using his left hand, he had tried to reach back and undo the D-ring holding the harness to the cord. Yet it only served to fling him around all the more. He'd dangled a good six feet over the ground. So he'd gripped the closest branch with his feet and tried again. This time the clip escaped him and he had collapsed on a branch that was, thankfully, thick enough to hold him.

As fast as his left hand allowed him, he'd removed the harness, then removed the long-sleeved Henley. Using one arm had been tricky but he'd managed. He had dropped down the rest of the way to the ground, draped the Henley over the top half of the fallen branch and covered the remainder of the log with loose branches. If Valentina had looked too closely he'd still have been found out, but he'd hoped the fog would force her to come closer. She'd need to investigate to be sure. If she approached the branch, it'd give him the advantage of surprise and hopefully he could gain control of her gun.

He had tensed behind the trunk, waiting to spring, but the lady had seemed squeamish. She'd merely waved the light over the area for the briefest of glances. He'd straightened. All that worry for nothing.

Now, Aria was inside. He needed to find out what they were planning to do with her and attempt a rescue without a gun. They wouldn't have likely taken her inside just to kill her. Or would they?

He picked up the nail gun. The plastic casing had busted. Great. If he survived, he'd need to pay a hefty chunk to replace that expensive piece of hardware too. More importantly, he was left without any weapon to help Aria escape. He shook his head and prayed for wisdom as he snuck to the back of the house.

Aria tried to clear her vision by wiping the tears away with the backs of her hands. Robert was in the kitchen, chugging liquid from a clear glass bottle. She had an inkling it wasn't water or soda.

"Take it easy," Kirill cautioned. "You've had enough. That should've taken the edge off." He opened a first-aid kit.

Robert slammed down the bottle with a big exhale. He turned toward the women, but only had eyes for Valentina. "Is he dead? The man who shot me?"

Aria's lips trembled, and she fought to keep the tears back. She could really use her emotional armor right now, but it didn't seem to be working.

Valentina nodded. "He's not going anywhere."

"Good," Kirill said.

"If you hadn't killed him already, I would've," Robert shouted.

Kirill ignored his boss's rant and wrapped several layers of gauze around Robert's forearm. "Almost done," Kirill said. "It's going to need a doctor's attention, though. You might need a tetanus shot after that nail."

"Put Dominic on standby. He can take a look at the wound as soon as we get back. Assuming the highway will be passable soon. Otherwise, they will send a boat as soon as it is safe."

"Still no phone service," Valentina interjected.

"Phone," Robert growled. "That's right. Check her phone. Let's see who she claims to have been texting."

Valentina rifled through Aria's purse and pulled out her cell phone. She didn't look at it but thrust it toward the men.

Robert took the phone with his good hand. He tapped the screen and clicked the power button a couple of times with him thumb before he threw it to the ground. "Of course." He looked at Aria, rage in his eyes. "Surprise, surprise. It's dead. As you will be if you don't tell me where you've put the evidence." Robert wrenched away from Kirill's tending. A dangling piece of gauze hung over the edge of his arm. Robert grabbed Aria's arm and squeezed tight. His fingers dug into Aria's triceps. She inhaled sharply and jutted her chin up toward the ceiling.

"You, my dear, are going to be in a lot of pain until the evidence is in my hands. And then it won't matter who you've told about the evidence, once it's already been destroyed."

Aria's steel reserve broke. She just didn't care anymore. What good would it do? He would still win. That much was obvious. "It's back at the other vacation rental."

He eased up on his grip and raised an eyebrow. "The place you stopped and stole clothes and food?" He laughed in her face. "Yes, I know you were there. Good. This is good." He shoved Aria back. She stumbled into Valentina, only causing Robert to smile more. He turned to Kirill. "It's not far from here. Let's go."

Inside the garage sat the familiar silver Hummer. Kirill took the wheel and within minutes they were on the road. Valentina held a gun at her side, but it was loose in her fingers.

Aria studied her. She still believed her first instinct—Valentina had been crushed by George's death; she had loved the man. So she must have reached the level of desperation to be number one in George's life if she was willing to place him in danger. It reminded Aria that the Bible said love was not self-serving.

Aria slumped in her seat. How could she judge Valentina when she had wanted something similar herself? Aria had wanted a love that held no risks, no sacrifice. She saw now what she really wanted was a love that was self-serving.

She dropped her chin to her chest. If only she could do it all over again. She was facing her own death, despite attempts to find a life without pain or remembrance of things that caused heartache. She had never been in control, despite all her self-assurances that she was choosing a better path in life.

Please forgive me, Lord. I was mad at You so I stopped seeking You. I stopped putting my hope in You. Please heal my heart. I want to be wise, but I also want to trust in You. If it's not too late, help me see a way out of this mess. Help me put one foot in front of the other, because I don't think I can go on alone. My heart is broken. I need You.

TWENTY-ONE

David's mind raced as he snuck up the steps on the back deck. He pressed against the siding next to the back door. He overheard Robert's threats and Aria admit where the evidence was stored. He wanted to yell at her to stop so she wouldn't give away their only bargaining tool, but he couldn't reveal his whereabouts yet. Not until he could think of a plan. The moment he heard the door to the garage close, he slipped open the back door and entered the kitchen.

A first-aid kit with gauze and a bloodied nail brad sat in the middle of the counter top. He cringed with the knowledge that he caused someone such pain but he was also sure the man would've killed him if he hadn't. Besides, he was sure a nail gun injury would heal a lot faster than the bullet wounds in his shoulder and ear.

David fingered the ball of gauze. If he took a minute to stop the blood loss, that'd probably work in his favor in the long run. He rolled it diagonally around his head so that it covered his ear but would hold without medical tape—of which he had none. He kept his eye on the door connecting the kitchen to the garage, in case they had forgotten something.

There was a gaping wound in the front of his shoulder. Since he was certain the bullet had entered from the back that meant it had ripped right through him. So there was a bullet loose in the construction area. He made a mental note to come back and find it, should they need it for evidence.

David took another roll of gauze and wrapped his shoulder the best he could, but it was a challenge with only one arm. He almost passed out from the pain when he tried to apply pressure. His dentist was likely to have some cracks to repair given how hard he gritted his teeth in the process.

Finally, he grabbed two travel packs of extra-strength acetaminophen from the kit, ripped open their wrappings and gulped the pills down without liquid. He was doubtful it'd do much good once the adrenaline wore off, but he hoped it would be better than nothing.

This house didn't have a fancy permanent generator. The lights were out. David smirked. If Aria were here, she'd have written a note to the owners apologizing for the window—no doubt leaving his phone number to come replace it—and warning them of the dangers of mildew without a generator. And it would've driven him nuts. It also would've made him laugh. Oh, how he loved that girl. And he needed to get her back…now.

He heard an engine start. The Hummer. David snuck through the living room and flattened his back against the door, so he could listen through the broken window. As he heard tires crunch onto the road, he dared a peek. The silver Hummer was disappearing into the forest. And if Aria handed over the location of the flash drive, he had no doubt what would follow.

David ran to the garage door. He used his phone

light, although its beam flickered from low battery. *Hold on just a little longer.* He strode into the garage and found only a mountain bike against the wall. So disappointing. It'd be almost impossible riding with his bad arm, although it'd be faster than trying to catch up to the Hummer on foot.

He shuffled through the items on the garage shelves. Fishing gear. He flipped open the tackle box and instantly found what he was looking for…a small serrated knife used for cleaning fish. If the owner was a true fisherman, David knew it'd be the sharpest tool in the house. He kept the safety guard on and slipped it in his pocket. Shiny metal next to it caught his eye. A Master Lock. He frowned. In a jam, it might have a use. He moved on, his mind tallying everything he'd seen in the garage.

David unsheathed the fishing knife and made his way to a hiking backpack he spotted hanging on the wall next to the bicycle. He sliced through the bungee cord material that weaved in an elaborate zigzag on the outside. It turned out to be one long cord, suited to his purpose.

He picked up the Master Lock and let it rest in his right palm—the one that caused him excruciating pain if he used it—as he set his left hand to work. He weaved and wrapped over and over until he had completed the monkey-fist knot over the lock. The knife had given him the idea.

Professional fishermen used to be fond of monkey-fist knots over weighted ball bearings. They used them as small anchors—the only problem being accidents happened too frequently. Fishermen would throw the weighted lines and unsuspecting crewmembers would try to catch them. The wrapped steel would pack a punch and seriously injure someone's hand or foot. In David's case, he would use it only if he had to keep them from hurting Aria.

Without electricity, there was no use trying the garage opener. The mechanism was already unlocked due to the men in the Hummer. At least that worked to his advantage. He'd never have been able to reach the red lever hanging from the ceiling.

David bent down and pulled on the door, grunting from the sudden throbbing in his shoulder. He couldn't afford to waste another minute. He screamed through the pain as the door finally opened. The smell of the pine soothed him, as it made him think of Christmas and family and love…and Aria. He had to save her, even if they had no chance together. He needed to be there for her.

He swung a leg over the bike when another glint of metal caught his eye. Inside the side pocket of the hiking backpack was a long tube. A spray of some sort with a picture of a growling bear. He slipped it out of its holding and his nose tingled just thinking of the pain bear spray could inflict on someone, but he'd take it just in case. The pulsing in his forehead caused a painful sensation behind his eyes. He took a deep breath and he started to see spots on the farther edges of his vision. *Lord, please help me not pass out. Keep Aria safe. Help police find a way here. Also, if You could keep black bears out of my way tonight, it'd be appreciated.*

Something nagged at the corner of his mind. He looked back into the garage, worried he might have forgotten something. It was so organized, so pristine.

The bear spray had been in the backpack, ready to go at a moment's notice.

"I wonder," he mumbled, and leaned over to unzip the hiking backpack. Inside were bottles of electrolyte replacement and granola bars. He moaned in relief.

"Blessed be the prepared hikers, Lord," he said aloud.

He chugged half a bottle of the chilled liquid, thanks to the January coastal temperatures. His taste buds didn't register the lemon-lime flavor until he was finished. He stuffed the bar in the pocket of his cheek, not wanting to waste another second. He could chew as he rode.

Unless Aria managed to divert them in route, she was leading the men back to the house where she'd stashed the evidence. David would need to stay on the main roads if he were to make good time. With a final breath, he pushed his legs into motion, the movement causing his shoulder to throb double-time. If he wasn't able to get them out of this situation soon, he wasn't going to be any good to anyone. He'd be dead.

It registered that the men were talking in the front seat but Aria wasn't paying attention to what they were saying. She was too busy straining her mind to figure out a solution. Despite her utter defeat, she wasn't ready to die. Her mother needed her and wouldn't be able to handle Aria's death.

Aria warred between giving them the evidence and facing the consequences of torture to fighting back somehow…but with what? Her peripheral vision told her that Valentina, slack-mouthed and staring out the window, was back in her comatose state of mourning.

If Aria had more time, perhaps she could convince Valentina to see reason, but they weren't alone now and she couldn't envision a scenario where the gunmen would allow such discussion.

If she could take Valentina off guard, maybe she stood a chance. One thing she felt certain. Those men would never find the flash drive if she didn't give up the location, and for a reason she couldn't pinpoint, she felt that fact would have made her dad, George, and David proud.

The Hummer pulled into the driveway. She cooperated with the men and walked in front of Valentina as they led the way around the side of the house. Valentina held the gun loosely, lazily. Aria was tempted to take it by force, but there was no place to run if she did. Six feet to the left was a steep drop-off and every other direction was either locked houses—she no longer had her purse full of credit cards to help—or gunmen. Her odds were dismal.

They entered the living room where only hours ago she had kissed David. She choked on a sob. She wished that their last interchange hadn't been full of heated accusations. It was a cowardly way to end a conversation, let alone a relationship. She could never ask for his forgiveness. The tears won.

Robert spun around and examined her. "There will be less crying if you show us the evidence."

She lifted her chin and gritted her teeth to keep them from chattering. "Because I'll be dead faster?"

He raised an eyebrow and stared at her for a moment. Then he laughed, as if her question was a joke. He lifted his hands, the gun cradled in his palm. "Why do you think I want to kill you? Do I look like a man who enjoys killing? No."

His questions deserved a sarcastic response, perhaps something cutting, about a gun in everyone's hands but her own, but she held her tongue. Time was her only ally, despite not having any assurances the authorities were getting any closer to reaching her.

Robert took a step closer so his nose was only an inch from her face. "I only use weapons when forced." He looked straight into her eyes. She tried her best to win the staring contest, but his breath reeked. She turned her face away for a moment. He grinned, pleased with her response, then straightened. "So do not force me, *kotyonok*."

Aria had suspected, but wasn't sure, that English was his second language, until he used a foreign term. She wanted to know what he had called her but she figured that was why he did it. He wanted her to ask. This was a game to him.

Robert pursed his lips and looked between her and Valentina. "We will take a look around," he said. "Make sure there are no surprise visitors waiting for us. Explain to her." Robert narrowed his eyes and glanced her way. "After that, there is no more waiting. Kirill has itchy fingers."

An involuntary shiver went up Aria's spine at Robert's last sentence. Kirill wouldn't be nice, she was sure of it. The moment the men rounded the corner she turned to Valentina. She had a better grip on the gun now, and was more alert since Robert's threat. "What do you need to explain to me?"

Valentina shrugged. "I'm not sure. They assume I think like they do, but I don't. I would prefer not to see you shot, Aria, so tell them where you hid the evidence. They won't be patient with you. Kirill was very angry, especially with you. His burns still hurt. He won't be nice. He'll make you suffer. Robert is unpredictable. He called you his kitten, but that doesn't mean much."

"Back at the other house you seemed sure they wouldn't kill you. Why?"

Her eyes widened. "We're family…extended family."

Aria thought about her first name and Kirill… Russian, as well? Hadn't David mentioned similar scams running through the Russian mob? "You can't really guarantee they won't kill me, can you?"

Valentina's lower lip trembled. "Just do what they say. It's your best chance."

Kirill walked back into the living room, his gun pointed at her. Robert was one step behind him. "The waiting is over."

Aria held her breath, hoping to build up courage. She'd need it more than ever to make her plan work.

TWENTY-TWO

David veered the bike onto the driveway next door to the blue house. He leaped off the bike and jogged to the side of the generator. He'd been debating his move the entire bike ride over. It helped him keep the focus off his burning lungs, legs and shoulder.

He ran to one of the windows he knew was part of the back bedroom, right behind the den. David slipped off the sheath of the fish fillet knife. After a steadying breath, he shoved the sharp blade between the top and bottom halves of the window, directly in the center. It slipped in easier than he imagined.

With his good hand, he wiggled the knife back and forward until the tip was touching the middle of the inside latch. He let go of the handle for one moment, then slapped it downward. The metal popped upward. The latch lifted up and over but only three-quarters of the way. So it was mostly unlocked, but not all the way. He removed the knife. Brute force was his only shot at getting the window open now. Only problem was his left shoulder was weaker than the right, and he still needed to be quiet. The element of surprise was his only hope.

The window gave way with a good shove from the heel of his left hand, but the screen still needed to be popped out. It was slow, methodical work that in reality only took two minutes, but to David it seemed like a lifetime. His intense workout schedule was saving him, and never had he been so glad for the discipline as it took a great deal of strength, especially with only one working arm, to lift himself up. He twisted his torso and maneuvered his way through the window.

David strained to hear voices. He heard a man mumbling and a female voice answering. He crossed the room and pressed his ear against the wall. *Please don't let me be too late, Lord.* The voices were on the move.

He put the knife in his right hand. The blade was slightly bent near the handle, but the serrated portion was still sharp. In an emergency, he knew he could throw it or use it for self-defense, but he hoped his homemade weapon would do the trick.

He slipped the wrapped lock from his pocket and dropped the weighted cord down to his side, taking care to ensure he had good grip on the end. He peeked out the doorway. The coast was clear. He stepped onto the wooden hallway floor.

"You win. As I've already told you, it's in this house," Aria said.

"And you are stalling," Robert announced, a smug grin on his face.

"Pardon me if I'm scared," she snapped. "I think I'm entitled. I'm not used to being held at gunpoint by a man who clearly wants to shoot me."

"Kirill, lower your weapon," Robert ordered. "Now,

see? This is just a business transaction. You tell me where the evidence is, and you will get to walk away. I'll let you run and hide somewhere else until the waters recede."

Even in the moonlight, Aria could see Kirill smirk and knew he would not let her get away that easily, despite Robert's promises. But what choice did she have, unless she was able to distract them enough to get Valentina's gun? Her best chance would be if they were focused on something else...something like the evidence. "It's in the garage," she said.

Robert stared at her a moment. "Good girl. Where exactly in the garage?"

"It's better if I show you," Aria replied. Her fingers were shaking. The reality that she was about to face possible death was too real. *Help me.* Peace, like the type she experienced when David had prayed for them in the woods, dripped down her like an anointing. Her fingers stopped trembling.

Robert tilted his head, and she wondered if the change she felt was visible to him. He held out a hand. "Lead the way."

Her steps were slow and methodical, as she hoped to gather up more courage on the way. They passed the kitchen, the stairway, the hall—a shadow in her peripheral caught her eye. She felt her eyes widen. The silhouette sunk back into a doorway...the door of the den they had hidden together mere hours ago.

"What is it?" Robert asked.

"I'm sorry. The crying catches me off guard." It wasn't a lie. She tasted the salty tears on her lips but hastened her steps to the garage, lest they got suspicious. Aria was so thankful for the dark. She couldn't stop smiling…and crying. He was alive! It had to have been him. And she needed to keep him that way. She just hoped he wouldn't interfere with her plan.

Turning the doorknob to the garage, she squared her shoulders. This time her armor seemed to return. Her reserve hardened. She flipped on the light and strode to the center of the room. Valentina and Kirill followed her inside, both squinting at the bright light, which caused them to grip their weapons tighter. Aria pursed her lips and pointed to the wall next to the workbench. "It's in there. You'll need a screwdriver to open it."

Robert stood in the doorway, his shoulder propping the door fully open. His left hand gripped his gun, which was pointed directly at her, as if he had expected her to try something and he wanted a quick escape, if needed. His eyes darted to the wall and then back to her. A broad grin spread across his face. "Well done. I'll admit it. We never would've found it." He thrust his chin at her. "So get a screwdriver and open it."

Her mouth dropped open. "Me?"

"Yes. Why not? You have no injury."

Aria's shoulders dropped. It was a major blow to her plan. She had figured that Robert wouldn't do it. He was the boss and had the injury to his forearm, and she had been sure he wouldn't ask Valentina, especially after finding out they were family. She thought Kirill would be the natural choice, and if he put his gun down or in his holster that would've given her the split-second advantage she needed to take away Valentina's gun and disarm them one by one. Or at least die trying. Now what would she do?

"I'm growing impatient," Robert said.

She dragged her feet to the workbench and shuffled through the tools, passing over the screwdriver a few times before finally picking it up. Making a grand display of wiping her tears away she looked over her shoulder at where everyone was standing. Valentina had moved next to her at the workbench, apparently taking Aria on as her responsibility. Kirill stood in the middle of the garage, legs spread apart in a fighting stance, watching her every move. Kirill was the biggest threat—he was ready for action. Robert was still holding the door open. Wait. Was there a shadow approaching?

Aria turned to the wall. If David had his own plan, she needed to keep everyone's attention on her. "The electrical joist box is one of the best hiding places because it is part of the house, a fixture if you will. When someone ransacks a house, they typically don't think to unscrew things that are physically part of the—"

A whoosh followed by a guttural scream swung her attention to the door, but before she could see what happened everything went black.

Aria made her move. She switched the screwdriver to her left hand, spun around to where she could sense Valentina was standing and slammed the screwdriver's flat blade onto Valentina's forearm. Aria used her right hand to twist Valentina's wrist three quarters of the way around, causing Valentina to drop the gun right into Aria's right palm.

Kirill made the same cry as Robert. What on earth? The light flipped on. Kirill was on one knee, his left hand over his stomach in anguish, but his gun was rising.

Without thinking, she cocked back the hammer on Valentina's gun and pressed the trigger. A bullet whooshed past Kirill's face, missing him by an inch. Kirill jerked back in surprise and something that resembled a small ball of yarn pelted him in the knee. Kirill howled and the gun left his fingers and soared until it hit the garage door. Robert was in the fetal position at the bottom of the step while David stood above him, holding the edge of the…yarn? She wanted to rush toward him but knew it'd need to wait.

Aria picked up Robert's gun and, while pointing them both at Kirill, approached his gun, only a foot from where he crouched. With the three guns in her possession, she felt she could finally look at David.

"Are you okay?" he asked.

He was breathing hard and fast, and his face was paler than his white T-shirt. His entire right arm was covered in reddish-black streaks. Blood. She gripped Valentina's gun tighter. "Help me get these guys secured before you pass out. Then I'll be better than great."

He nodded, but even that seemed to take a great effort. David was gripping his cord contraption hard while holding a jagged black knife in his right. She moved to him and pulled out the zip ties she remembered he had stored on the side of his tool belt. In exchange she put the two other guns in the belt.

Within moments, she had the three gunmen's wrists bound. David pressed the garage opener, and she waved the gun toward the Hummer, indicating they should get in. Kirill glared at her. "You think I should be scared of a little girl with a gun?"

She sighed. Some people really were slow learners. She straightened her arm and shot the front tire of the Hummer. The hefty tire's air pressure made a loud noise that took her slightly off guard. It served her purpose, though. Kirill's eyes widened, and he walked forward. She ordered Kirill to crawl in the trunk, Robert got the middle and a sobbing Valentina got the front passenger seat. She retrieved her bag from the floorboard and slung it diagonally over her chest. Then she took six extra zip ties and tied their original bindings to the door handles, as well as bound their feet together.

David was starting to shiver violently.

"David! Go inside."

He didn't respond. Was he starting to go into shock? She jogged over and turned him toward the inside of the house. "It's okay now."

She pulled David into the kitchen, and loved that she was able to flip on the lights without fear. "You saved me, David."

Again, no response. His eyelids were dropping. She led him to the couch. "Lie down, honey." She put her hand behind his head and gently pressed on his chest until he cooperated. She found some throws and draped his frigid body. She examined the wet gauze around his shoulder. "You've lost a lot of blood." She put her hand on his face. "Stay with me, David. I can't lose you now." She stuffed a throw pillow underneath his feet then ran to the bedroom closet to grab more pillows.

"Come on, come on," she scolded herself. First-aid training 101 went over shock treatment. What should she do? She racked her memory. She needed to elevate his legs…six inches or twelve inches above his head? In this case he had lost so much blood, she decided more had to be better.

By the time she came back to the room his eyes were closed. She placed the pillows under his legs and grabbed his wrist. Her fingertips pressed hard, searching. His pulse was there. Faint, but still present. His shoulder didn't seem to be bleeding anymore, but she shoved another pillow underneath to elevate it above the heart as well.

"I love you," David whispered, but his eyes were still closed.

Her heart sped up. She grabbed his hand and kneeled down beside him. "I love you, too. David. Can you hear me? I was just scared to admit it."

Impossibly, he smiled. "I know. It's a great comfort to me to know you can't hide your feelings from me."

She wanted to slap his chest. This was the David she knew and loved—the one who wouldn't let her get away with anything, who challenged her in every way to be a better person. "I missed you."

"I know."

She laughed. She couldn't help it.

"I missed you too," he added. "Aria?"

"Yes?"

"I kind of wish you wouldn't have shot the tire."

"We can't go anywhere, anyway," she objected. "There's no way out yet."

He groaned. "I think I need a hospit—" His voice faded and his mouth went slack.

"David? David?" She found his phone in his tool belt and powered it up. It had one red bar left. She pressed the contact for his father.

David needs hospital now. Shot. Pls help.

She held the phone and bowed her head. "Please send help, Lord."

A moment later the phone vibrated.

Give location. Will get to you no matter what. Do your best and give him our love.

The phone beeped at her. Only one percent battery left. "No," she shouted and sprinted to the porch to get the address. She typed in the address, pressed send and a moment later the phone went black. Aria gripped it tightly and prayed the message had gone through.

She returned to David. At least he was still breathing. She knelt down on her knees and held his hand and prayed.

TWENTY-THREE

It took effort to open his eyes, and the light was blinding. Someone tried to pull Aria away from him. He reached out for her.

"David, she's fine. Aria, wake up. For crying out loud, I'm not trying to hurt either of you!"

He knew that voice. He squinted to see a tall man in front of him. "Dad," he groaned.

"Hi, son," his dad answered. Dad's voice was extra stern, with a wobble. David hated seeing his dad scared, because he knew if there was fear in that man it meant things were bleak. "You just save your energy for staying alive, David," his dad continued. "We can talk later."

Aria was bleary-eyed and trying to stand up. "I… I must have fallen asleep."

Dad chuckled. "You were down for the count. I can't imagine what you two have been through."

David was suddenly aware there were two other men in the room, preparing a stretcher. Another man moved David's extremities around, examining him, but he didn't have the strength to look and see what he was doing. The pain intensified and he growled.

"Mr. McGuire, we have the two gunmen and an accomplice strapped inside the Hummer outside. They killed George and shot David," Aria told his father.

"The Portland police have an air unit on the way as well. I'll let them know. Are you ready to leave?"

"Oh!" Aria shouted. "The flash drive! I just have to get it and I'll be right there."

David wanted to scream as the medics lifted him off the couch and carried him to the stretcher. The pain threatened to knock him unconscious. His eyes flashed open as he took a giant breath.

"Give it a second. We just injected your shoulder with morphine. We need to take you on a little trip to get you in that helicopter."

In an instant, they were shuffling out the back door and Aria rushed to his side. "I have the evidence, and you're going to be fine. You have to be fine, understand me, David McGuire?"

"Yes, ma'am."

Her eyes left his face, and her expression morphed into surprise.

He twisted his head to look in the direction she pointed. The sunrise was breathtaking but also shined light on the wreckage below. There wasn't a single building on the conference center campus left standing. Movement caught his attention. He strained to hold his head up as the men carried the stretcher farther away from the view. A short distance away, a group of whales blew little jets of water up, so close together it reminded him of a synchronized fountain.

"It's a reminder," his dad said. "That life goes on. Don't worry, Aria. They'll fix David up. They'll fix this town up. One foot in front of another." He laughed. "Literally. Come on. Let's get you two out of here."

David smiled and let his eyes close, knowing Aria was in safe hands. A moment later, he heard what sounded like metal scraping against metal. His eyelids felt weighted down, but he sensed someone very close to him. "Did I wake you?" Aria asked. "I'm sorry. How do you feel?"

"Beat up," he muttered, feeling as if his mouth was full of sand. He blinked and realized he wasn't in the helicopter. He was in a hospital room. She offered him a giant flexible straw attached to a cup the size of a pitcher. He took a tentative sip. "I don't remember the helicopter ride. What'd they give me?"

She shrugged. "I don't know. You haven't been out of surgery long."

"I've been in surgery?" He looked down at his shoulder and realized it was numb. That was probably a blessing. His ear still throbbed, however. He reached up and found a hard, smooth cup covering it with gauze in the middle of it. His fingers trailed the textured fabric up and around his head.

Aria stood up and showed him her phone, on the camera setting, so he could use it as a mirror. "You don't look your best, but you're still as handsome as ever." She bit her lip. "They had to do reconstructive surgery on your ear. Between your gun wound and that, you might be here a while." Her curls bounced, framing her face. Her eyes looked bright and more green than brown in the hospital lighting. She inhaled. "I've already answered all of the questions the authorities could think of, so hopefully they'll give you a break for awhile. And your dad helped me track the vacation rental owners and the ATV owner to make sure we reimburse them properly. So there's nothing for you to worry about. Your job is to rest and get better."

He laughed. "I have no doubt you've taken care of everything." Aria was always on top of the details. "You've had a shower," he accused.

Her eyes widened. "Busted... I also took a nap." She fidgeted with the hem of her pink blouse. "I figured if you were resting..."

"It's only fair you sleep too, right?"

She laughed and reached for his hand. The moment they touched her expression sobered. "When I thought you were dead," she whispered, "I realized all the time we had wasted because of my fear—"

"—and my fragile ego," David interrupted. "Aria, you have no idea just how much I want us to be together, but I need for you to be sure. A hundred percent." He shook his head slightly. "It hurts to admit it, but my heart can't take losing you again, so I'm going to keep my guard up until you're sure."

"I am," she insisted, and gave his hand a squeeze.

"Aria," he murmured, "take some time. It's what you asked for two years ago and I messed it up. These last twenty-four hours have been the most intense of my life. You need to grieve—really face it—and then if you are sure you're ready to do life with someone like me, I'll be ready."

David didn't say the rest of what he was thinking, but if she took some time and still said she loved him, he was willing to leave construction behind if that was what it would take to be together. He hoped and prayed that wasn't what the Lord or Aria would ask of him, but after seeing men intent to kill her, he realized his career dreams paled before finding love. "If you still feel this way, I'll be waiting with open arms." He followed her gaze to his shoulder wrapped up tight. "Well, with one really wide arm."

She smiled but her eyes filled with tears. "I know you're probably right, but after being without you for so long, I never want to leave your side."

"Which is why you have to. You need to be sure." He looked up to see his parents in the doorway. "I'll be well taken care of. Go."

She leaned down and kissed his cheek. A surge of wellbeing rushed down his spine. Although the pain medications could've played a part, he still preferred her kisses.

Aria spun around with a nod toward his mom and dad, and walked out of the room. David hoped he hadn't just made a stupid decision, and prayed she wasn't walking out of his life forever.

It had been six days since she'd last spoken to David. His mom had sent her update texts about his condition. If all went well, he should be given the green light to check out tomorrow.

Aria took a deep breath, the opened padlock in her hands and reached down to lift the tin door to the storage unit. The movement stirred up a gust of stale, dusty air. She covered her nose with one arm, allowed the dust to settle again and entered the unit filled with furniture and boxes.

Like a magnet, she was drawn to the chocolate-colored couch recliner against the wall. As a young girl, she'd sat on the armrest while her dad asked her about her day. As she grew older, she sat on the matching couch, which was placed perpendicular to his chair. But it was always the same routine that brought her comfort. She sat down and patted the armrest. In front of her was a tower of boxes. The second one from the top caught her eye. The movers had labeled it Girl's Room Documents with black marker. She stood and shifted the boxes until she could place it down in front of the recliner. She rocked forward and opened it.

Inside, the box was filled with school papers, her Bible, a half-empty box of tissues, several pens and notebooks, and a stack of unopened envelopes that filled the majority of the box. The sympathy cards. Aria took a deep breath and, after stacking them on her lap, began opening them one by one.

The first three cards were exactly what Aria feared they'd all be. A generic "With sympathy" signed with nothing but "Sorry for your loss." This was the precise reason her mom wanted nothing to do with these cards, as well. But the fourth card surprised her. It was covered in ink on three sides of the card. Written by one of her dad's longtime crewmembers, it relayed his experience as a new hire, when he'd spent his evenings staying up late with friends only to fall asleep during each work break. Her dad had grown exasperated at having to wake the man when he was late getting back to work, so one day Dad had carefully glued a flimsy watch to the man's forehead. To the crew's amusement—and her dad's chagrin—the watch had stayed on the man's forehead for a full week until someone suggested using fingernail polish remover. Aria laughed until her side ached. Why hadn't Dad told her that story?

On the backside of the card the employee related a different account, this time from ten years later. His little boy had just been diagnosed with cancer and he had caught her dad trying to sneak away after stuffing a giant envelope filled with cash into the employee's mail slot. Aria placed a hand on her heart. This was also the dad she knew.

Card after card told stories of her father—some she'd heard, some she hadn't. The next card stopped her in her tracks. It was a card with scripture. Romans 8:38-39: "For I am persuaded, that neither death, nor life, nor angels, nor principalities, nor powers, nor things present, nor things to come, nor height, nor depth, nor any other creature, shall be able to separate us from the love of God, which is in Christ Jesus our Lord."

Her vision grew blurry but she still stared at the verses. David was right, she had been running from grief, but that was only partly correct—she'd really been running from love. From his love, her friends' and family's love, but mostly from God's love. She'd been stuck, afraid that if she let them love her, she'd be forced to move on with life, and that would hurt even more. Tears rushed down her face. *I need Your love, Lord.*

Peace draped over her again, a warmth that spread from the crown of her head down to her spine. And after an hour, she was so thankful the movers had packed everything—even an empty candy bar wrapper and her half-filled box of tissues—because the tissues were almost gone now.

Except…no card from David. It'd be a lie to say she wasn't disappointed.

She lifted her Bible out of the box and brushed off the dust. Sticking out of the Psalms was a pink envelope. The verse in the middle of the page caught her eye: "What time I am afraid, I will trust in thee." The envelope shook in her hand. "Why do I get the feeling You're trying to tell me something?" she asked the Lord.

She took a deep breath and gently opened the envelope and pulled out the card. It wasn't anything like she imagined. It wasn't covered with hearts or romantic sayings. Instead it was homemade. David had taken blueprint paper and drawn little cartoons of what he imagined their life together would be like. Her fingers drifted over the thick, soft paper, and she craved a pencil to be able to add to his plan. She had been kidding herself. Architecture wasn't her father's dream, it was her own, and she missed everything about it.

She opened the thick paper and a shiny ring fell into her lap. She gasped.

Aria,
I wanted this letter to be eloquent and something you could treasure, but I'm not one for flowery language. I have tried to show you how I felt, albeit sometimes poorly, ever since you steered that kite straight into me. It may have scarred my head, but you have branded my heart. I love you, Aria, more than I can express with a pen and paper. I want to spend the rest of my life with you. This ring may not be real, but if you're willing to wear it as a symbol of our future together, I hope to replace it with something that will stand the test of time.
Hopeful and forever yours,
David

Aria fingered the ring. On closer inspection, she could tell the princess-cut diamond was made from either glass or cubic zirconium, but it was still beautiful. She slid it on her fourth finger and imagined what a marriage to David would be like. As a tremor of fear clutched her, she fought it back with the words she'd just read. Nothing could separate her from the love of God, and because of that, she could love others fully even with the risk of losing them.

Aria looked around the cluttered storage. She had three sudden desires: to deliver the cards into the hands of her mother whether Mom wanted them or not, to visit her father's grave and to see David in the hospital.

Fifteen minutes later, she found her mother wasn't at home, which was odd since Aria had borrowed the sedan from her. Aria left the cards in a pile on her nightstand. After a stop at the flower shop, she pulled into the parking lot of the cemetery. She hadn't visited the gravesite since the burial.

She stepped out of the car and tightened the belt around her long raincoat. The skies released a frequent drizzle that often accompanied January afternoons.

Cradling the small pot of begonias into her elbow, she walked the path bordered by dogwood trees until it opened up to thick grass. In the back, the cemetery was lined with oak trees. Her mother said they had made sure to buy a plot that matched their anniversary so it'd be easy to remember. December 27. Twelve lines back, twenty-seven spots over, next to the thickest tree.

She counted the lines, but as she grew closer she noticed a man in a navy-blue jacket with a white diagonal stripe and a matching hat on top. His shoulders were broad but hunched over. She really didn't want to have step past another mourner. It was such a personal, private thing. Yet as she got closer she realized the stripe was actually a sling, and the man was in front of her father's plot.

"David?"

He turned toward the sound of her voice. It *was* him. She shifted the pot of flowers to her left arm and ran to him. The wet grass flicked droplets on to the back of her legs but that didn't slow her down.

"Aria?"

"I thought you were still in the hospital," she cried. She tried to slow down but the slick glass had its revenge. She lost her footing, and if it weren't for David, who took a large step and righted her with his left hand, she'd have slid into him as if he were home base.

David continued to hold his wide stance and squeezed her upper arm. The gold flecks in her eyes danced with the light coming through the tree branches. "Are you okay?"

"Safe," she said, triumphantly.

He cocked his head.

She flashed a breathtaking smile.

"You're beautiful," he said, not able to help himself.

Aria bent over to pick up a dropped pot filled with flowers that resembled small roses. She straightened. "Thank you." Her voice was softer, more vulnerable.

"Um…were you here to…?"

He nodded. "Pay my respects. Since I missed the funeral."

"There was no funeral."

"What?"

She shook her head. "Dad put in writing he didn't want a funeral. He didn't want a dime going to what he thought would be a boring event where everyone was forced to pretend he was a great guy."

"But he was a great guy," David protested, meaning every word.

She laughed. "And I think Dad knew he was, too. It was an excuse." She sighed. "He didn't want friends and family spending money to come to it and he wanted any life insurance money to go fully toward providing for my mom."

David nodded. He could understand the reasoning. "Would you like some privacy?"

She nodded. "In a bit, but since you're here I wanted to give you something. I had planned to come visit you next." She slipped her hand into her right pocket and withdrew an envelope. "For you." She looked at his chest and frowned. "You can't open it. Sorry. I'll do it." Aria took out the card and placed it in his hand.

It was made of blueprint paper. Was she giving back the card he wrote? Except this was different. He studied it and flipped it to see the inside. "These are…part of your designs for a conference center?"

When they had dreamed about it together on the beach all those years ago, he had no idea she had been serious enough to draw up designs.

"I found them in storage today. I wouldn't have gone there without your push."

He only half heard her response, as he had already started reading the note.

David,
If I had opened your card two years ago I would
like to think I would've responded the way you
hoped, but I can't be sure. I'm confident of
my response now, though. You challenge my
strength and weaknesses equally, all to be the
best person I can be. But when I mess up, you're
also encouraging and compassionate.

David skimmed past her list of all his "amazing"
traits. He didn't want to think on them because he
didn't deserve the praise, but he hovered over the last
words and took time to digest them.

I love you and I want to be with you, forever,
God willing. I will cherish each day with you
and, with God's love, know that I can handle
whatever comes our way.

He looked up to see that she had walked away to
give him privacy to read the card. She set down the
flowers next to her father's gravestone and exhaled
slowly, a look of peace on her face. She turned her
gaze to him, tears in her eyes, but the light reflected
off her hand…her hand? David felt his eyes widen.
She was wearing the promise ring from the envelope.
David cringed inwardly. If he had a chance to lecture his younger self, he'd tell him to show up at her
doorstep with the real thing and tell her straight, like
a man. She didn't seem to be embarrassed at the fake
diamond hanging off her finger, though. She was willing to accept him, as goofy as he was.

David stepped forward and reached for her. With

one hand, he pulled her close to him and as her face tilted up, he brushed his lips against hers.

"I don't know exactly how it will work," she admitted. "I don't want to be long distance again, but I want to finish my semester if they'll even let me and—"

David grinned and pulled her tighter to him despite the zing up his forearm. "About that, I just had coffee with your mother and asked her for her blessing—"

Her pocket vibrated at the same time it released a series of chimes. "Uh, hold that thought for just a moment. This might be Mom." She pulled the phone out of the raincoat and pressed it against her ear. "Oh." Her eyes widened. "Okay. Sure. When?" She slipped her phone back in her pocket, and stepped closer to him. "You were saying?"

His cell phone chimed. He frowned but took a glance at the caller ID. Aria leaned over to see for herself. "It's George's lawyer," she announced. "That's who called me."

"Then I'll call back later." He reached for her hand. "Aria, I love you." He squeezed her fingers slightly as the skies erupted with a downpour.

She lifted her chin and smiled while blinking away the raindrops. "I love you too."

He stepped closer, hoping his tall form would shield her from the rain. He bent down and gave her a soft kiss. God was teaching him to be patient.

His question could wait for the right time.

TWENTY-FOUR

Twelve months later

Aria stared at the dapper man in the tux standing beside her. They faced the ocean side-by-side, one of the few braving the chilly beach. The crash of waves against some of the large boulders on the shoreline provided a soothing rhythm that lulled her into quiet reflection. It seemed to have the same effect on David.

The rest of the guests had all left the heated tent attached to the newly built conference center. She looked down at their hands intertwined, the white gold band visible on her fourth finger. The breeze drifted over her neck, playing with a few of the loose tendrils that had escaped from her updo. She may have been tired both physically and emotionally, but the contentment and joy in her heart kept a smile on her face. The sun began its final descent behind the horizon and offered them a magical display of colors to gaze upon. She nestled closer into David's side.

"Are you ready for your wedding present?" he asked.

"Wasn't my ring enough?" she wiggled her finger but he didn't let go of her hand.

"Nope." He flashed a half smile but his eyes were bright, the telltale sign that he was up to mischief."

She narrowed her eyes but her mouth wouldn't co-operate, still stuck in a wide grin. "What are you up to?" she pressed.

"I hope you don't mind, but we won't be staying in the lodge for our honeymoon like we planned."

She felt her eyes widen. "David, we worked so hard to have it finished in time."

He titled his head from side to side, his expression thoughtful. "True…but there might have been a secret, second construction project going on at the same time."

He gently tugged on her hand. "Come on." They walked past the lodge and he led her on the new path that connected the center to the gardens. A couple of bouncing animals caught her eye. "Wait. Is that…?" She bent down. "I can't believe my eyes. The bunnies are back."

David chuckled. "They probably didn't want to miss the wedding." He raised an eyebrow. "And they're not my gift to you." He moved her along to where she knew he'd kept his truck and camper and construction trailer. Except they were no longer there. In its place sat…an octagonal cottage. Her eyes widened with recollection. "The captain's quarters." She turned on him, which was hard to do fast in a wedding dress, even with the train detached. "How'd you hide this from me?"

"I made sure we had enough vehicles here, kept the blinds down on that side of the trailer on the rare occasion you'd stop by during your last month of your internship. Plus, I knew you wouldn't want to stay long anywhere near the line of Dumpsters."

She laughed. "I do have a sensitive nose, don't I?"

"And that's probably why my brothers chipped in and bought me a lifetime supply of deodorant for our wedding gift."

She giggled. "They're so thoughtful."

He led her to the front door. "Do you want to do the honors?"

"You're not going to carry me over the threshold?"

He patted his arm. "Old shoulder injury."

Odd. She'd seen him working along with his men without complaint, but she didn't mind—he must be as exhausted as she. The doorknob clicked under her touch to reveal an open living room and kitchen area. To the left, she spied a bay window facing the ocean, and to the right...

"My dad's chair," she cried. Past the wood floor entrance, thick white carpet like the one she envied in the vacation rental prompted her to kick off the jeweled sandals she wore. He'd built her dream home. She let her toes sink into the carpet and picked up the frame sitting on the end table. "It's the letter from George," she whispered. George had left an envelope for them at the reading of his will. A week after the fact, she had asked the lawyer's office if she could have the letter but the receptionist claimed it was lost.

Aria let her finger drift over the glass as she reread words she hadn't seen for a year.

David and Aria,
I consider you both part of my adoptive family.
I am blessed to know two people who love this

campus as much as I do, and if possible, have a greater vision for it to bless others. If you're reading this, then it means it's time for you two to oversee it. I don't know whether or not the Lord has opened your eyes enough to see you're made for each other. I hope you have seen, but if for some reason that is not the case, I still leave the estate for you to do with as you will.

With love,

George Swanson

The Lord bless thee; and keep thee: the Lord make His face shine upon thee, and be gracious unto thee: the Lord lift His countenance upon thee, and give thee peace.

Aria replaced the frame gently and was about to tell David how much she loved the gesture, but her attention was diverted by a bookcase that lined the entire wall. "We have some book hunting to do," she murmured.

He nodded. "Later, perhaps." David reached for a remote and she expected him to show her a widescreen television he'd decided to install, but instead he clicked a button and the bookcase split apart. The two sides swung open and revealed a master bedroom.

"It's gorgeous," she murmured. She pointed at him. "You used my secret passage design."

"Guilty," he said, grinning. "Your dad's chair wasn't the only thing I found in storage."

She looked up and spotted her teal-and-black-colored stunt kite hanging from the back of one of the bookcase sides that presumably served as bedroom walls when closed. She marveled at it until the back of her knees felt pressure and gave way. Her feet kicked up and she screamed as she found herself in his arms. Aria tried to catch her breath, laughing, delighted at the surprises of the day. She patted his chest. "Mr. McGuire, what about your shoulder injury?"

David titled his chin so they were face to face, his eyes darkening. "I may have exaggerated. Timing hasn't been my strong suit in the past but I've been working hard at it. Are you ready to be carried over the threshold, Mrs. McGuire?"

Aria put both hands on his face, enjoying every minute she was in his arms. "David, with the Lord by our side, I'm ready for anything."

* * * * *

Dear Reader,

When I visited the coast of northern Oregon with my family, it quickly became one of my favorite places in the world. On the way there, my children listed all the things they hoped to experience. They wanted to see an elk, see a shark, touch a starfish and find an unbroken sand dollar. I laughed at the first two hopes, but it only made my youngest pray harder. And wouldn't you know it—every single one of those things happened. (Shockingly, a young shark washed up onto the shore. Right at our feet. Rescuers arrived immediately.)

During this amazing visit, I was struck by the number of tsunami warning signs and evacuation route maps. While I pray a tsunami never hits that area, if it ever does, I hope that all the planning and preparation keeps everyone safe, as it did in my fictitious town.

While the beauty and majesty of the setting inspired me to write *Surviving the Storm*, so did my frequent habit of assuming. It's so easy for me to think I understand the intent and motivation of things said and done by my loved ones. I wanted David and Aria to wrestle with this. Their understanding of each other is tainted by pain, pride and their own experiences. Once hurt, without seeking resolution, it's easy to go down a slippery slope. Thankfully, David and Aria turned to God and found peace and love. I wish the same for you.

Blessings,
Heather Woodhaven

COMING NEXT MONTH FROM
Love Inspired® Suspense

Available September 1, 2015

THE PROTECTOR'S MISSION
Alaskan Search and Rescue • by Margaret Daley
As an Anchorage K-9 police unit sergeant, Jesse Hunt regularly puts his life at risk to rescue others. But he'll pull out all the stops when a bomber threatens his hometown—and his former high school sweetheart...

RODEO RESCUER
Wrangler's Corner • by Lynette Eason
Tonya Waters isn't about to fall for another cowboy bull rider, yet when handsome Seth Starke offers help escaping her recently freed stalker, she'll accept. She barely eluded the assailant before, and now he's after Tonya *and* Seth.

PLAIN THREATS • by Alison Stone
Ever since her husband's crimes left Rebecca Fisher an Amish widow, she's been targeted. To discover whether her stepson knows more than he lets on, Rebecca turns to his professor for answers. But the questions put them *both* in danger...

DESPERATE ESCAPE • by Lisa Harris
Former special ops agent Grant Reese is trained to defuse land mines—not rescue damsels in distress. But when Dr. Maddie Gilbert is kidnapped by drug traffickers, he'll face any threat to save the woman who's always held his heart.

EASY PREY • by Lisa Phillips
US marshal Jonah Rivers has never forgotten his brother's widow, Elise Tanner. When he finds her in a dire situation—with a nephew he didn't know existed—he'll stop at nothing until they're both out of harm's way.

EXPERT WITNESS • by Rachel Dylan
Tasked with protecting a sketch artist who is testifying in a high-profile murder trial, US marshal and former FBI agent Max Preston jumps into action to keep Sydney Berry safe. But can he save her from the secrets of her past?

REQUEST YOUR FREE BOOKS!

2 FREE RIVETING INSPIRATIONAL NOVELS
PLUS 2 FREE MYSTERY GIFTS

Love Inspired®
SUSPENSE
RIVETING INSPIRATIONAL ROMANCE

YES! Please send me 2 FREE Love Inspired® Suspense novels and my 2 FREE mystery gifts (gifts are worth about $10). After receiving them, if I don't wish to receive any more books, I can return the shipping statement marked "cancel." If I don't cancel, I will receive 4 brand-new novels every month and be billed just $4.99 per book in the U.S. or $5.49 per book in Canada. That's a savings of at least 17% off the cover price. It's quite a bargain! Shipping and handling is just 50¢ per book in the U.S. and 75¢ per book in Canada.* I understand that accepting the 2 free books and gifts places me under no obligation to buy anything. I can always return a shipment and cancel at any time. Even if I never buy another book, the two free books and gifts are mine to keep forever.

123/323 IDN GH5Z

Name _____ (PLEASE PRINT) _____

Address _____ Apt. # _____

City _____ State/Prov. _____ Zip/Postal Code _____

Signature (if under 18, a parent or guardian must sign)

Mail to the **Reader Service:**
IN U.S.A.: P.O. Box 1867, Buffalo, NY 14240-1867
IN CANADA: P.O. Box 609, Fort Erie, Ontario L2A 5X3

**Are you a current subscriber to Love Inspired® Suspense books
and want to receive the larger-print edition?
Call 1-800-873-8635 or visit www.ReaderService.com.**

* Terms and prices subject to change without notice. Prices do not include applicable taxes. Sales tax applicable in N.Y. Canadian residents will be charged applicable taxes. Offer not valid in Quebec. This offer is limited to one order per household. Not valid for current subscribers to Love Inspired Suspense books. All orders subject to credit approval. Credit or debit balances in a customer's account(s) may be offset by any other outstanding balance owed by or to the customer. Please allow 4 to 6 weeks for delivery. Offer available while quantities last.

Your Privacy—The Reader Service is committed to protecting your privacy. Our Privacy Policy is available online at www.ReaderService.com or upon request from the Reader Service.
We make a portion of our mailing list available to reputable third parties that offer products we believe may interest you. If you prefer that we not exchange your name with third parties, or if you wish to clarify or modify your communication preferences, please visit us at www.ReaderService.com/consumerchoice or write to us at Reader Service Preference Service, P.O. Box 9062, Buffalo, NY 14240-9062. Include your complete name and address.

LIS15

Lydia closed her eyes and tried to relax. But visions of
the bombing assailed her mind. The sound of hideous
laughter right before the bomb went off. The expression on
Melinda's face when she knew what was going to happen.
Was she alive? The feeling of helplessness she experienced
trapped under the building debris. Her heartbeat began to
race. A cold clamminess blanketed her.

Her hospital room door opened, pulling her away
from the memories. When Lydia saw the person who
entered, her pulse rate sped faster. Jesse Hunt. She wasn't
prepared to see him.

He looked as if he'd come straight from the crime
scene. As a search and rescue worker for Northern
Frontier, he'd probably work as long as he could function.
The only time he'd rest was when his K9 partner, Brutus,
needed to.

So why is he here?

He stopped at the end of the bed. "Bree told me you
were awake, so I took a chance and came to talk to you."

His stiff stance and white-knuckled hands on the railing betrayed his nervousness, but his tone told her he was here in his professional capacity. Saddened by that thought, Lydia said, "Thank you for finding me."

"I was doing my job yesterday."

"Knowing the people who would be searching kept my hope alive. Have you found everyone?"

"We don't know for sure. Names of missing people are still coming in. I was hoping you could tell me how many people were in the restaurant when the bomb exploded."

"I don't know…" The thought that the bistro was totally gone inundated her. She dropped her gaze to her lap, her hands quivering. Emotions crammed her throat. She turned for her water on the bedside table, but it was too far away. She started to lean forward and winced.

Jesse was at her side, grabbing the plastic cup and offering it to her.

She took it, and nearly splashed the water all over her with her shaking.

Jesse steadied the cup, then guided it to the bedside table. "I know this isn't easy, but anything you can remember could help us piece together what happened. We've got to stop this man."

"Nobody wants that more than me. I'm sure I'll remember more later." She hoped she could.

She needed to.

Don't miss
THE PROTECTOR'S MISSION
by Margaret Daley,
available September 2015 wherever
Love Inspired® Suspense books and ebooks are sold.

Love Inspired

Love the Love Inspired book you just read?

Your opinion matters.

Review this book on your favorite book site, review site, blog or your own social media properties and share your opinion with other readers!

Be sure to connect with us at:
Harlequin.com/Newsletters
Twitter.com/LoveInspiredBks
Facebook.com/LoveInspiredBooks

HLIREVIEWSR